CW01391089

About the

The Move is Sharon Reid's debut novel. Currently living in the Chilterns, Buckinghamshire, she has always enjoyed writing and is a keen photographer. She enjoys travelling and whilst on a holiday a few years back with her husband, Andy, they both witnessed some strange and unexplained happenings within the cottage that they were staying in. These somewhat disturbing events gave her the idea and the inspiration for this book.

THE MOVE

Sharon Reid

THE MOVE

Vanguard Press

VANGUARD PAPERBACK

© Copyright 2025
Sharon Reid

The right of Sharon Reid to be identified as author of
this work has been asserted by her in accordance with the
Copyright, Designs and Patents Act 1988.

All Rights Reserved

No reproduction, copy or transmission of this publication
may be made without written permission.
No paragraph of this publication may be reproduced,
copied or transmitted save with the written permission of the pub-
lisher, or in accordance with the provisions
of the Copyright Act 1956 (as amended).

Any person who commits any unauthorised act in relation to this publication may be liable to criminal prosecution and civil claims for
damages.

A CIP catalogue record for this title is available from the British Library.

ISBN 978-1-83794-783-6

This is a work of fiction. Names, characters, businesses, places, events
and incidents are either the products of the author's imagination or
used in a fictitious manner. Any resemblance to actual persons, living
or dead, or actual events is purely coincidental.

Vanguard Press is an imprint of
Pegasus Elliot Mackenzie Publishers Ltd.
www.pegasuspublishers.com

First Published in 2025

Vanguard Press
Sheraton House Castle Park
Cambridge England
Printed & Bound in Great Britain

Dedication

For my husband Andy, My daughters Steph and Sophie and my two grandsons Bobby and Zac. In loving memory of my dear parents Robin and Betty.

Acknowledgements

Thank you to my family for all their support and encouragement.

PROLOGUE

Father John sat motionless in his meagre cramped kitchen. The old-fashioned period features which were usually so inviting, now seemed frigid and stark. Icy breath exhaled from thin, pursed blue lips, pitiful shoulders slumped into a sullen hunch. His eyes darted hastily around the room and towards the creaky wooden door which led to the narrow hallway. He wasn't alone. The dark eerie presence enveloped the air around him, encircling and entwining like a mysterious ghostly mist.

Once again, he began to question his faith.

CHAPTER ONE

A singular beam of piercing white light penetrated its way selfishly through the only gap in the heavy linen curtains, precipitously landing on the hanging mirror. I squinted abruptly, burying my head into the warmth of the duvet. Briefly closing my eyes, I contemplated what the day and, in fact, the future had in store for us.

My mind raced around in circles, frantically reasoning with its apprehensive inner self. I stretched my long legs until a cramp rudely interrupted, breaking my gentle effort of rising. Wearily, I pulled back the comfort of the duvet. It was going to be a profoundly long day.

Standing in front of the window, I pulled open the curtains and peered out. It was six o'clock, and the morning already had a beautiful, bright autumnal crispness about it. The trees were desperately hanging on to their final leaves, a splendid array of red, golds and russets. Everything looked so wonderfully surreal and perfect. Then the feeling of forbode swiftly returned.

The practical clothes that I had laid out the previous night were arranged neatly on one side of the sealed, packed boxes, all efficiently itemised and ready for their final destination. I dressed with haste and ran downstairs, glancing around wistfully. Our home looked so forlorn, desolate and almost alien now; our lives in impassive cardboard boxes, ready to embark on the passage ahead.

The kettle rattled noisily as it boiled, interrupting my unhappy train of thought.

I placed the coffee cup on the empty bedside cabinet, nudging my husband affectionately, as I perched down beside him. He turned over, yawning and stretching noisily.

"A big day for us," I whispered softly, sighing and frowning simultaneously.

"Everything will be fine," he gently reassured, pulling me close, his arms enveloping my tense body. Momentarily, for a brief split second, everything felt good again.

The removal lorry and its two brusque men arrived, and showing zero signs of any emotion, they began the task of fulfilling their assignment. I watched as our life's belongings and memories were hoarded onto the cold, stark truck without the slightest piece of compassion. I stared at our beautiful furniture being taken from our happy home. Apprehension shivered through my body, as tears gently fell from the lakes forming in my eyes. I didn't care what I looked like; I was hurting inside and aching for something I no longer had ownership for.

After what seemed like an eternity of torture, my husband slowly turned the key to lock our front door for what would be the final time. He turned, taking hold of my trembling hand, and we stared at each other knowingly. We walked down the path towards our overloaded car, embarking on our new chapter, a picture-perfect cottage in a charmingly quaint village, somewhere for us to create new memories.

CHAPTER TWO

I didn't look back as we drove slowly away. I choked down a painful tear which was then instantaneously replaced by cascades trickling down my already flushed cheeks. Deeply I inhaled, seeking to regain my composure. It worked, and I hurriedly brushed away the invading tears.

We barely spoke as we drove somewhat detached to our new destination, the scenery becoming increasingly more picturesque as the miles quickly passed us by. The moors seemed endless and mysterious, with wild horses grazing so carefree. Some galloping, their flowing manes whipping out behind them, they looked jubilant and defiant all at the same time. The bright, autumn sunshine cleverly captured the golden tops of the gorse bushes. I smiled to myself. Capturing a glimpse of my face in the wing mirror, I felt positive once more.

Another hour soon passed, and Mark pointed out a rickety road sign. We were ten miles away from our journey's end. I felt a tight nervous knot in my stomach which instantaneously disappeared as I began to recollect our reasons for moving in the first place.

We had stumbled upon the historic medieval village whilst enjoying a romantic break in a quaint bed and breakfast somewhere along the Dorset Coast. On our second day, we had walked for what had seemed like miles. In desperate need of some sort of refreshment, we made a detour from the unending woodland track after seeing a National Trust tourist sign featuring the Castle logo. We traipsed our way up the steep hill which led us into the village. I gasped as I stared in awe at the road leading gently through cobbled streets, charming little shops and an elegant dovecote which all stood in the shadows of the menacing castle, towering unashamedly in the backdrop like the village keeper. It had literally taken my breath away.

At the top of the cobblestones, an imposingly gothic-looking hotel stood magnificently in its proud position. A display board outside advertised 'Excellent food', a welcome offer which we could hardly resist. On entering the grandiose doorway, we stopped momentarily to take in the commanding structure and decor of this monumental building. Dark beams covering both ceilings and walls seemed to almost be groaning with the strain of upholding this exquisite framework. An opulent fireplace took a defying centre stage in the palatial entrance.

We sat in the beautifully landscaped garden of the hotel, soaking up the glorious sunshine. Together we ate huge doorsteps of sandwiches, and we drank the traditional regional cider whilst taking in the astoundingly breathtaking views which were completely enveloping us. It was there and then we started our love affair with the beauty and ambience of this stunning place.

Thereafter, we visited as often as feasibly possible, staying at the hotel. We took it upon ourselves to get to know the local shopkeepers and residents, and on every visit, we were always very warmly welcomed.

It was on one of these increasingly more frequent occasions, when we were enjoying a strong coffee in the exquisite little café situated next to the calming waters of the River Avil, we decided wholeheartedly to sell our home in London and start a new life in the place we both had come to love so much.

There began our painstakingly long search for our ultimately perfect property. After numerous disagreements, pointless bickering and delicate soul searching, we finally agreed on a quaint three-bedroom cottage oozing character and charm. The property was situated on the main road leading out of the village and was near perfect in every aspect. We had argued about the fact that it had been on the main road, and the huge front window open for people passing to blatantly stare in, but eventually found compromise on the basis that nearly everything else met our strict criteria.

The heavily beamed ceilings featured prominently in every room; original and traditional fireplaces were hugely in abundance. The unique cold stone floors throughout the downstairs were strangely appealing, and we both fell in love with the old stable door which opened out to the mysteriously private and surreal courtyard garden surrounded with beautiful shrubs, hidden secretly away in little nooks and crannies. It was our ultimate dream come true.

We secured the property at a surprisingly low price and sold ours for a substantially hefty profit. The entire conveyancing process went fleetingly smoothly, and before we knew it, we had completed on the property that today was to become our new home.

CHAPTER THREE

I turned and smiled at Mark as we embarked onto the steep tree-lined drive into the village.

"Home!" we both said simultaneously before bursting into laughter.

The dominate castle and its breathtaking grounds shrouded in mystery, greeted us like we were old friends, still totally imposing and as majestic as ever. We entered its envelope of corporate hospitality. Our car slowly mastered its way through the cobbled high street. The picturesque shops were still bustling with activity, the delicatessen selling off the last of its fresh produce. Aromas of freshly brewed coffee wafted its way through our open windows, so we stopped at the rustic Italian café and ordered cappuccinos.

The removal men were approximately forty-five minutes behind us, giving us a brief moment to gather our thoughts and appreciate the coffee. I quickly ran to the delicatessen and grabbed a fresh baguette, together with a selection of cold meats and cheese, something to satisfy us later as the hours ahead were going to be manically hectic and a test of our sanity.

Mark found me, and with a beaming smile spread across his face, he jangled a set of keys in front of me. "It's all ours now," he said, smiling. "Let's go."

We almost ran to the car. Momentarily, I felt anxious again, butterflies uncontrollably wavering around inside me. Was it excitement, trepidation or anticipation? I couldn't tell any more. All I knew for certain was, this was it: our new life was about to begin.

As we pulled up onto the gravelled driveway, I stared intensely at our new home, and for a split second, the sallow greyness of the cottage exterior shocked me.

"We definitely need to give the outside a paint; it looks worse than I remember." I continued, "Either a cream or a white shade would be nice, and we could have hanging baskets, candles in the windows." I gabbled on enthusiastically, "I really want blinds, although it would spoil the front, we could—"

"We have plenty of time for that," Mark expertly interrupted before my verbal cascade got any worse.

With the car parked in its new home, we stepped out onto the narrow pavement, and pausing briefly, we stood back to take in and fully appreciate the picture in front of us. The sun was shining amidst the clear blue skies. We both simultaneously inhaled deep, nervous breaths as the keys were inserted into the outer door of the cottage.

Apprehensively, we stepped into the white porch-like area before opening the main heavy oak door. It creaked loudly like the splintering of wood, virtually squealing under the duress as we pushed it gently open.

Our cottage smelt musty and slightly damp, which was obviously to be expected; it had remained empty for four years prior to us purchasing it. The previous owners had only stayed in its residence for five short months, apparently suffering marital problems, then fleeing somewhat abruptly and without notice. I had discovered this information from the little old lady in the village bakery, who'd nosily enquired on our purchase, curiously wishing me all the luck in the world.

Entering the stone-floored reception, I stared slowly around. The neglected cottage felt unloved, practically depressed in its current empty void. It was almost as if it was waiting for us, waiting to be filled with the love and devotion that it so rightly deserved.

Interrupting my thoughts, the loud rumble of the removal lorry was heard as it pulled up closely outside, a huge black shadow darkening the deep front window, like a heavy raincloud waiting to burst. A sharp tap on the outer door swiftly followed, and quickly the onslaught of the moving in process began.

Both of us were completely stressed out and utterly exhausted by the time the last box had been arranged in its relevant room. We had frantically arranged furniture where we had initially planned, even if only on an interim basis until we were more certain. Beds, dining table and our sofas were in their chosen designated spots.

In the front main bedroom with its creaky and crooked dark wooden floor, I had made up our bed, with its crisp, newly purchased bed linen, so that in the very least we could sleep comfortably. The kitchen had been scrupulously scrubbed clean and was now fully laden with all our utensils, both new and old. Other possessions still neatly packed in their boxes could wait until the morning.

We bade a grateful farewell to the hardworking removal duo who literally hadn't stopped since their early arrival that morning, proving right the excellent recommendation that had been given to us and working like mad dogs in the last of the rapidly fading light.

"Let's take a walk up to the hotel and have some dinner," Mark said.

I fervently agreed, and hurriedly, we both scrubbed up so that our shabby appearances looked somewhat acceptable to the outside world.

Closing the doors behind us, we walked slowly along the narrow pavement until we reached the cobbled high street. The view up to the hotel never failed to amaze me. The historic yarn market which in Norman times would trade wool was spectacularly lit up. The old-fashioned, black lampposts lined the streets like tin soldiers standing on parade.

We reached the hotel and stepped into the intimidating arched doorway. Immediately, the glowing embers of the fire welcomed us, inviting us into its warm and cozy atmosphere. We located an intimate table for us in a snug corner, and I sat down as Mark made his way to the bar, quickly returning with a large glass of Sauvignon and a pint of Guinness – an extremely well-deserved reward for all our hard labour during what had been a long, emotionally demanding day.

Reflecting on the day's events, we chatted happily whilst relishing our drinks. Our eyes quickly skimmed over the varied menu, and we made our choices of steak and ale pie and lasagna. Our meals arrived swiftly after ordering, much to my husband's relief; he was absolutely ravenous, and we ate in a surreal silence, savouring every single delicious mouthful.

Finishing, the friendly young waitress efficiently cleared our table as we sat back in total appreciation. Deciding to have another drink before heading back to our new home, we sat relaxing for a while longer, acknowledging the ambience of the gracious hotel. An hour later we were opening the door of our new home for the second time that day.

"That's late for children to be up and running about," I remarked as we entered the front reception. I had heard muffled sounds of children's voices and what had sounded like the patter of tiny feet. The faint noises appeared to have emerged from the upstairs of the next-door adjoining cottage and had stopped almost instantly.

"I didn't hear anything," Mark responded as he yawned wearily. "Let's go to bed. It's been a long day." He gently took hold of my hand and led me up the creaky old staircase.

CHAPTER FOUR

It was a peculiar night's sleep. I must have woken over a dozen times, disorientated and not knowing where on earth I was. Mark, however, had blissfully snored his way deafeningly through, oblivious to my somewhat unsettled and disrupted slumber. The cottage had creaked and groaned tirelessly, making my hair stand on end at even the slightest murmur. I found my inner voice strictly chastising, telling me everything was normal including the endless volley of strange sounds.

After tossing and turning, I resentfully decided to get up. Walking along the chilly wooden hallway towards the bathroom, I glanced upwards and noticed that the second bedroom door at the rear end of the cottage was wide open. It had been shut the night before, of this I was certain. The bedroom was directly opposite ours on separate ends of the lengthy hallway. I walked up to it and jerked it closed. The door itself wasn't easy to manage as the wooden flooring in that room was extremely uneven and so irregular it snagged gratingly along the bottom. I turned back and went to the bathroom.

Mark followed shortly after having woken from his undisturbed sleep. We ate a light breakfast sitting at our table nestled cozily in the front window. Opposite us was a pretty picture postcard cottage, pale yellow in colour with an abundance of brimming hanging baskets, honeysuckle-laden trellis and pots bursting with colourful displays of flowers. It was still relatively early, so everywhere was quiet other than the odd random car driving fleetingly past.

The morning was spent unpacking the remainder of boxes, hanging up our clothes, loading the drawers and generally transforming the cottage into what we could call our home. Our family photographs placed all around added homely.

familiarity. We had decluttered considerably when packing up our previous house, thus making our move so much simpler.

Later that day, we drove a few miles into the neighbouring town, a popular seaside resort with a small but vibrantly busy harbour filled to the brim with local fishing boats. The sandy beaches which occupied positions either side of the harbour walls were an entirely different place in the summer months as was the town with numerous streams of tourists spending their days building sandcastles, expertly navigating the surf, consuming ice creams from the abundance of sellers and spending extortionate amounts of money in the cascades of flamboyant arcades covered in gaudily lavish baroque decor.

Out of season, like any seaside resort, the town was an exceedingly better place, subdued and tranquil with just the locals going about their day-to-day business. The plentiful souvenir gift shops shuttered up during the stark winter months, having made all the money they needed during the swamped high season.

A brief walk along the seafront and backing the sand dunes was another reason Mark had been enthusiastic for our move. A stunningly spectacular golf course with striking views of the turquoise ocean took pride of place in its ostentatious seaside resort, and being a keen golfer, the course was an obvious added bonus.

On the opposite side of the harbour, a row of vividly brightly coloured beach huts uniformly lined the boundary of the beach; privately owned and generally passed down through the generations, families and friends frequently able to enjoy their summers year on year. Seldom would any become available for purchase, and if on the extremely rare occasion one did, they would be sold at an extortionately greedy premium.

I had taken glorious photographs of these huts capturing copious images of various weathers and seasons, and each time the results were more astounding than the last. I could never tire of them.

We visited the busy supermarket on the borders of the town and stocked up on more or less everything we needed as shopping in our quaint little village, however charming, was considerably more expensive.

After our frivolous spend, we loaded the car before having a placid stroll into the village centre. With the overloaded tourist season safely out of the way, the town boasted quietness. All of the shops were still open at the moment; however, as soon as one would close its doors for the oncoming winter, the others would swiftly follow like a nimble domino effect.

We stopped at an exquisite pavement café and ordered coffees and a Danish pastry. Sitting outside, we made the most of the beautiful autumn sunshine. There was a slight breeze, which also gave a distinct nip into the air. We were warmly dressed, so it didn't matter.

I turned to look at Mark, his handsomely strong features never failing to disappoint me, his silvery almost white hair always immaculately groomed. He was a tall man and athletic in build. I had always loved the fact that he had towered over me; it constantly made me feel safe and protected. His icy blue eyes were like the turquoise waters of the Caribbean, and his firm jawline complete with fashionable stubble completed his suave look.

We had fallen in love almost immediately, never wanting to let the other out of mind or sight. Second marriages for both of us, we gave each other everything both physically and mentally, appreciating and realising all the needs and requirements of the other. Initially, I had encountered a few teething problems during what was to be a difficult and trying period of adjustment; the trials and tribulations of introducing a new partner into my daughters' lives. We managed to get through it together, and my two beautiful grown-up girls eventually accepted Mark into their worlds.

Their father, my ex-husband, had unfortunately passed away at the terribly young age of forty-four. Suddenly, and terrifyingly unexpected, an aneurism resulting in sudden heart failure had killed him instantly.

There followed a tough and tenacious few years in which our daughters struggled to come to terms with their father's cruel and untimely passing. We had parted company a few years prior to this, but it still came as an appalling shock for us all to deal with, and very important that I kept his memory alive.

Eve, twenty-two years at the time, kept everything inside her, never wanting to talk about it; silence prevailing above all. Momentarily, every so often her grief would manifest, and her emotions would come flooding out like a volcanic explosion, its fountain of lava endlessly gushing out from deep within its crater. She worked as a barmaid. Academic was one thing Eve was not. She did what she had to do to get by and with a healthy inheritance was able to buy a comfortable house, her meagre earnings covering the monthly bills.

Eighteen months later, Eve, decided unexpectedly that she would join her talented boyfriend Tom who was a resident DJ based in Ayia Napa, carving herself a new interesting life in the balmy sunshine of the Cypriot Isle; working as a barmaid in the gyrating clubs and overly glamorous bars during the vibrantly, ostentatious summer season, then spending much of the bleak winter months and, more importantly for her, Christmas back in England. She was blissfully content, and although I missed her terribly, I eventually became used to the fact that she was no longer five minutes around the corner. We spoke as often as feasibly possible; Eve was happy, and that was the most important thing.

Jennifer, on the other hand, was an extremely troubled and vulnerable sixteen-year-old who put herself and me through a gloomy roller-coaster ride of emotional emptiness and sorrow. Losing her cherished father at such an impressionably young age was a bleak ordeal to say the very least. She had just started sixth form and within a couple of weeks found it all too much, together with unhelpful, non-communicate teachers and the total lack of understanding from the school in general; and finally to my utter despair, she dropped out.

A week or so later, she successfully applied for an apprenticeship with a well-known chain of hair salon. She came home on her first day proudly wearing her smart uniform bearing the bold company logo. I was overjoyed and so elated for her. Unfortunately, once again, these brief feelings were not to last. The rigor and constant bullying by a couple of senior members of the team was all too much for her vulnerable self to cope with, and on a sombre rainy Wednesday afternoon, she walked out, cascades of tears flowing down her reddened cheeks.

There on followed the drunken, disorderly nights, emotions all too often running high and having a field day each time they reared their sometimes-ugly heads. I found myself cursing her innocent dead father for abandoning me and leaving me alone with no support to deal with all this continual trauma and anguish. We cuddled, shouted, cried and somehow managed to scrape through each drama, hoping once again it would be the last.

My troubled youngest then passed her driving test first time. I cried silently at work when I received her call as it

29

bought home the fact that her father wasn't there to share her jubilant news. With some of her inheritance, she decided, obstinately against all significant advice, to purchase a brand-new Mini Cooper S, which she absolutely worshipped. Jennifer loved the fact it gave her newfound independence and freedom. She would think nothing of taking herself and her friends off to places even I wouldn't have felt comfortable driving to.

Regrettably, as I was beginning in a bizarre kind of way to expect, this albeit good news was not to last. On a Sunday morning at five a.m., I received a telephone call from a PC Stone.

"Is that Ms Lee?" his unattached deep voice questioned. "Ms Ann Lee?"

"Yes," I replied in a weak whimper, feeling both sick and faint simultaneously.

"We have your daughter Jennifer in custody," he continued in a mundane, somewhat bored, done-this-before voice.

"What has she done?" I almost screamed, sheer frustrated panic enveloping my body at an alarming rate.

"That information cannot be released to you by myself as your daughter is over eighteen. I will pass the phone over to her now."

It felt like an absolute eternity before Jennifer's subdued voice came on to the line.

"What have you done?" I cried hysterically.

"Drunk driving," came her short-dejected reply.

"How could you have been so utterly stupid and irresponsible?" I screamed out in sheer frustration. "Not only could you have killed yourself, you could have killed someone else!"

"I'm so sorry, Mum." She kept apologising, with me continuing to berate her until I slammed down the phone in utter disappointment and excruciating pain. Tears rolled down my cheeks. I sobbed uncontrollably until I physically couldn't cry any more. I ached inside, blaming myself, blaming my ex-husband, blaming life. I was totally inconsolable.

Pulling myself together. I called my sister, the one person whom I could constantly rely on, and broke the news. A short time later, my brother-in-law arrived. We took an eternal sombre car journey to collect my chaotic, unmanageable daughter from the prison cell.

Eventually, she walked out with jet black mascara streaks trailing down her ashen white cheeks. Dressed in her black attire from the night before, she looked almost Gothic-like with her raven hair stuck flat to her head like a roman helmet. No words needed to be spoken; it had all been said.

As we pulled up outside our house, Jennifer's Mini, her ultimate pride and joy, sat forlornly on the driveway. My brother-in-law had thoughtfully retrieved it from its abandoned place literally only two minutes away, so near yet so far. She took one sideways glance at it and burst into a deluge of fresh tears. That was the end of that, the start of which was to be eighteen long, punishing months.

Mark interrupted my reminiscing. "Shall we get a refill, love?" He stroked my cheek affectionately.

"That would be lovely," I eagerly replied. I was beginning to feel a slight chill but was relishing the peace and solitude of my own thoughts.

He went to reorder as I quickly slipped back. The dark void Jennifer felt over the following few months was punishment enough, seeing her car sat motionless every day, constantly reminding and silently torturing. Things finally calmed down after that disastrous episode, and I think it was the concluding wakeup call that was so desperately needed; maybe ex-husband was finally looking down on us, despite all my overwhelming and undeserving irritation felt towards him.

Jennifer, thankfully, resumed her studies and worked part time at the local pub, which she enjoyed immensely. She had fortunately inherited a practical two-bedroom maisonette from her father, which was only a five-minute walk away; so when the time was right for her, she moved in with her new serious boyfriend Jamie. It wasn't so much as an upheaval for me as she was just around the corner. It was during this time that Mark had unexpectedly entered my life, and we enjoyed multiple romantic dates getting to know each other.

I broke away once again from my train of thoughts and looked over at him. I smiled contently to myself, as he made me feel so fulfilled. We had a wonderful future ahead of us.

CHAPTER FIVE

We arrived back at the cottage, not realising quite how late it had become. Quickly, we unloaded our seemingly endless stream of heavily laden shopping bags from the car.

I noticed the patter of tiny feet running around next door as we stepped inside. The sound stopped almost abruptly as we dragged the groceries in from the cold porch entrance. We both unpacked and bickered as I kept rearranging items that Mark had tried so helpfully to put away.

A boisterously loud tap on the front door interrupted our innocently harmless squabbling.

"Wonder who that is?" Mark said as he walked out from the kitchen to the front door. I followed hurriedly behind him.

"Hello there!" said a cheery elderly voice. "My name is Freida, and this is my husband, Albert. We live in the cottage next door." She pointed in the direction of the property on her right.

Her husband, a short and extremely round man, stepped forward enthusiastically with an outstretched chubby hand. "Pleasure to meet you both!" he warmly greeted, thrusting forward a bottle of red wine as he did so.

"Hello, I'm Mark, and this is my wife, Ann," Mark responded as he welcomed them into our new home. We opened the bottle of wine that the elderly couple had so kindly bought and sat listening to their charming friendly chatter.

Freida, herself a slight woman in her eighties, hardly let her timidly meek husband get a word in as she constantly fiddled with her round spectacles and patted her neatly compact, grey bun. She told us that they had lived in the village for what seemed most of their lives and that our cottage had once been the 'Olde Village Sweetshop' which would explain the appealingly large window at the front. I pictured the window laden with rows of sweets as she continuingly spoke.

"What's the family like that live in the cottage that side?" I enquired, nodding my head towards the wall on the left.

"No one lives in that one, pet; it's been empty a fair few years now. How long would you say that one's been empty, Albert?"

"I'd say eight or nine years, give or take," Albert somehow managed to stammer before Freida fervently carried on.

"Same as this place. This was derelict for a few years until you came along. It will be nice to have some neighbours again." She continued to gabble on at an alarming pace. I wasn't listening to her conversation now. I was totally distracted, my mind racing around in frenzied circles. I had distinctly heard children playing there, running about and laughing. I sat motionless, staring numbly at the white stone adjoining wall on the left-hand side of the cottage. I felt strangely unnerved.

We bade Freida and Albert a relieved farewell. She had promised, passionately, to bring some freshly made jam tarts for us in the morning, and we politely said thanks as we waved them off.

As soon as the door had closed, I turned to Mark. "I definitely heard children next door, Mark!"

"Well, you heard the old folks; it's been empty longer than this one had." he acknowledged with an exasperated, impatient sigh.

"I know what I heard, Mark!" I snapped resentfully, angry with his peeved response.

Mark got up and came back with another glass of wine. We sat watching the TV in a stale, stony silence. I went to the kitchen to prepare our dinner and to escape to the solitude of my own thoughtful space. We had been a little extravagant whilst shopping earlier and brought some expensive salmon fillets, which I neatly wrapped in foil, seasoned with lemon juice and fresh parsley, before popping them into the warmed oven.

Out of the corner of my eye, I fleetingly saw Mark pass the kitchen doorway and go into the main lounge at the rear of the cottage. Washing my hands quickly, I followed him into the room to ask him something. I glanced swiftly around; he wasn't there. Confused, I walked back to the front room, where there he was, still prominently sat in the same, unmoved position, eyes transfixed to the vast TV screen.

"Did you just go into the other room," I enquired puzzledly.

"No, why?" he questioned, obliviously sipping his drink.

"Oh, no reason; I just thought you had, that's all." I returned, disillusioned to the kitchen, thinking to myself that I must be going completely and utterly bonkers.

The salmon smelt delicious as I gently served it onto a warm plate. We had buttery new potatoes with healthy, fresh green beans and sat at our candlelit table for two. I felt strangely unsettled and very agitated as we began to eat whilst, remarkably, managing to sustain a cheerful conversation between mouthfuls. Slowly, my unease began to subside.

We watched the TV for a short while more before locking up the doors and turning off the lights. Wearily, we retired upstairs to the comfort and warmth of our bed.

The next morning came far too quickly as far as I was concerned. Surprisingly, I had managed to sleep soundly and peacefully. Unusually, for me, I felt no obligation but to just lay there in the warmth of my own tranquil solitude. There was an empty void on Mark's side of the bed. I could hear him clattering around downstairs in the kitchen in a man kind of way. The radiators and their persistently abrupt clanging put a swift end to my peaceful awakening.

I glanced at my watch, almost eight thirty; unexpectedly late for me. I gently rose to go to the bathroom. Once again my gaze fell upon the open door of the top bedroom. Mark must have opened it, I thought, as it had definitely been closed the night before. I yanked it firmly shut. That room always felt so distinctively icy, despite the ancient, rickety radiators being on.

I dressed quickly, after a painfully lukewarm shower. We desperately needed to replace the boiler; it was a relic of a heating system and was on the rapidly increasing list of jobs to be done. Swiftly, I made the bed, before going downstairs. I walked down the creaky staircase, picking up my tan-coloured leather handbag from the cold stone floor on the way. I paused momentarily; I was certain it had been left it in situ on the sofa the night before. Shrugging my shoulders, I rummaged around the deep compartments finally, locating my mobile phone. I checked for any new messages from the girls, a habit which would never go away. There were none.

Mark handed me a mug of strong tea. "Morning, gorgeous. Did you sleep well?" he asked as he kissed me gently on the cheek.

"Hmm, I actually slept really well; did you?" I replied, sipping at my steaming hot tea.

"Not too bad. I woke early, so decided to get up rather than toss and turn, and I've mended a few bits here and there!" He smiled, obviously pleased with himself. "Do you fancy a nice walk today? It's lovely outside."

"Yes, let's; it's far too nice to be stuck indoors. I will make us a nice breakfast before we go," I replied enthusiastically.

We had scrambled eggs on wholemeal toast, seated at our exquisite sweet-shop window. Passers-by would glance in and quickly look away again as they were met with our two faces reflecting innocently back at them.

Some would politely acknowledge us, others would turn quickly away, cringing in embarrassment at the fact they had been captured staring obtrusively into our private world.

I cleared the table, and we both put warm layers on. Although the sun was shining, there was a sharp wind that in the shade would make it feel significantly cold.

We shut the old cottage door. I glanced up towards our bedroom window; the curtain seemed to slightly move. I momentarily looked away and then back up again; it remained still and motionless. Mark rattled the door, making sure it was fully closed and secure.

We walked towards the Water Mill, prettily nestled on the scenic riverbank, and then on towards the enchantingly dainty, thatched yellow cottages, covered with an abundance of radiant climbing roses filling the air with their intoxicating perfumes, their lustrous, picture-perfect gardens enclosed by uniformly neat white picket fences.

I stopped to take a photo of the astonishingly delightful display of colour filling my lens. Photography was my one indulgence, an expensive hobby that I had participated in for many years. My Nikon gave me overwhelming pleasure and escapism and very rarely left my side.

Continuing on, we walked along the leafy lane. The magnificent backdrop of trees looked stunning with their wonderful array of russets, reds and golds, making the most of their exuberant coats before being stripped entirely naked for the stark and cold winter months that lay ahead.

We continued onwards towards Gallows Bridge, a medieval 15th-century, narrow stone bridge, built during olden times for the packhorses to gain entry to the village and its imposing keeper, the castle. Built over a wide yet shallow river, brimming with pockets of tiny minnows, it was a fun, safe place for children and their parents to wade in their wellington boots or barefoot, weather dependent, carrying their buckets and fishing nets hoping for a catch.

From this ancient bridge, you could take in fully the grandiose of the hauntingly majestic castle situated in its elevated position on the densely wooded hill, a defiant protector of its village, preserving the past and future generations.

I took a few varied photographs of the trickling stream and its quaint bridge, then of the elegant medieval fortress. I had numerous pictures indoors but never stopped gaining pleasure from taking it at a different angle, light or season.

We carried on upwards towards the wooded glade and made our way nervously through the farmer's field of irate cows, blatantly irritated at the two annoyingly brash individuals that had invaded their precious privacy. Clambering over the half-rotten wooden stile, we climbed the sharp incline of the steep hill, my calves burning as we reached ahead for its torturous peak. Mark was panting heavily, like a dog gasping for water. I cursed myself for not being fitter.

Eventually, and after a hard painful slog, we arrived at the top. The view around us was breathtakingly surreal. Standing side by side on one of the many viewing platforms of the castle, we took in our spectacular surroundings. The sea and its glistening blue hues were sparkling like a bed of diamonds in the distance.

"Wow, what a view!"

I said the same thing on the numerous occasions that we had climbed to this spot. We giggled a mutual understanding. We took unhurried time to fully appreciate the stunning sights, before trudging our way back down, until we arrived at the outer edge of the castle perimeter. We then followed the trickling stream along, admiring the gigantic Gunnera plants adorning the edges of the riverbanks, their vast leaves overhanging and dipping the surface of the rippling water.

We crossed over the lovers' bridge where underneath, cascades of miniature waterfalls tumbled into the next one. Venturing through the true lovers' knot gate, we walked until eventually we arrived at the foot of the castle. The phenomenal and overpowering presence of the castle walls never failed to astound.

The grounds of the castle were beautifully landscaped and filled with the ostentatious violet and pink rhododendrons and hydrangeas, the vivid fuchsias and the beautiful scent of the magnificent magnolias. Admiring the radiant gardens as we casually passed through, I stopped periodically for more photo opportunities. Mark, taking full advantage of these brief interludes, would light up a small cigar.

We strolled through the equally imposing gatehouse which returned us back to the village centre and its two hundred listed buildings.

"Let me treat you to lunch at the hotel or rather dinner. Blimey, is it that time already?" Mark said as he glanced at his watch whilst wrapping his strong arm around my waist, pulling me next to him. I agreed, looking forward to the warmth and food that the hotel had to offer.

Negotiating the extreme unevenness of the cobblestones and passing the old yarn market on the left, we arrived at the hotel, where we received the usual warm welcome from the loyal staff. We sat in our usual cozy, intimate corner. The thickset mahogany panels that lined the walls always made it seem so dark, but at the same time, the gentle flames of the fire added to the extremely romantic atmosphere and aura of the grand dwelling.

Mark ordered our drinks, and we discussed animatedly our plan of action in regards to the long exhausting list of things that needed attention.

"Tomorrow, we need to source a heating engineer, electrician and decorator. The heating system has to be totally replaced, new boiler and rads; might as well install a new bathroom at the same time," Mark informed me enthusiastically.

"Yes, I agree," I replied. "Let's just get it all over and done with at the same time."

"The kitchen, I think, can wait for the time being..." Mark paused thoughtfully. "It's not too bad, and we could look at replacing it in a year or so."

"Why not do it straight away? We can afford it, Mark." I continued, "We came away from our sale with much more than we anticipated, and with this being our final move, we should make it the home of our dreams, don't you agree?"

"Let's arrange for the contractors to give us their estimates, plans and ideas; then we can make our decision from there."

We chinked our glasses in mutual agreement and then proceeded to discuss our food options from the menu.

"I fancy the fish with a jacket potato; what are you going to have?" I asked, still looking at the menu. "Don't tell me, steak and ale pie?" I joked playfully. Mark was a pie and mash kind of man, and after his long hard ramble today, he would most certainly need filling.

He looked at me, and we burst into simultaneous laughter as he really didn't need to answer; his face said it all!

CHAPTER SIX

As we reached the cottage after our enjoyable meal, I peered nervously up at our bedroom. The curtain was blatantly pushed over to one side, and most definitely not in the position it had been when I'd looked up at it in the morning. I felt excruciatingly queasy, wishing at that point that I hadn't eaten.

As we walked in, the patter of tiny feet ran away again.

"Mark! Did you hear the children?" I almost pleaded.

"No?" came his quick bewildered reply.

"Oh, I must be imagining things!" I retorted huffily.

We walked in, and immediately, I noticed our wedding picture, which I had carefully placed in the centre of the period fireplace, lying face down on the stone floor, glass fractured into hundreds of tiny pieces all around it.

"Mark!" I shrieked almost hysterically. "Look!" I was pointing drastically at the broken frame abandoned on the floor.

"Oops, it's fallen off! Don't worry, we can buy a new frame." Mark replied in a nonplus manner. "It's okay," he said as he bent down to gather what he could before retreating to obtain the dustpan and brush.

Taking stock of the bizarre situation, I felt strangely unnerved. What was going on? Confusing questions were doing somersaults in my mind. I went upstairs and made a point of looking up at the top bedroom; the door was closed. For a somewhat curious reason, I felt selfishly smug.

A little calmer, I changed out of the days dirty walking attire and ran a hot bath. Filled to the brim with fragrant luxurious bubbles, I sank deeply down, resting beneath the sealed envelope of warmth.

I caught a fleeting glimpse of Mark's shadow in the corner of my eye. "Hey, sexy, are you peeking at me?" I flirted playfully. Nothing. I called again, "Mark?" Once more there was no response.

I sank into the hot water, my long blond hair flowing like a mermaid in the deep depths of the sea. Closing my green eyes, I switched off, letting my body relax, the warmness of the bath making my skin tingle pleasantly.

After vigorously drying myself off, I wrapped myself in my fleecy baby pink dressing gown, the plush material feeling delightfully cozy next to my body.

I heard a knock at the front door. Mark answered it, and Freida's shrill voice echoed loudly in the hallway. She'd bought the jam tarts that she had promised us the night before and was a little disappointed that we hadn't been there in the morning when they had been freshly baked from the oven.

I heard Mark offering his sincere apologies before explaining that we had been out walking for the day. He eventually bade her farewell, ushering the little old lady quickly out of the door.

Switching my bedside light on, I clambered into our sumptuous bed, pulling up the king-size duvet. I was grateful that the coldness of the covers had been taken away by the snugness of my fleecy attire. I reached out for the book which I had briefly started reading. Barely a few pages in, I quickly lost interest. The move to our new home had by far taken precedence, and I found it increasingly difficult to concentrate on anything else.

The light bulb annoyingly dimmed itself before glowing almost fluorescently. I flicked the switch on and off again which seemed to have worked as the light now remained constant. I proceeded to start the same page for the second time, not recognising any of the paragraphs which I had previously supposedly read.

Mark entered the room; he undressed, joining me in our warm and cozy bed. The light offensively flickered again.

"The bulb needs replacing," I said as my husband gently lent over me to turn it off.

He took hold of my still unread book and placed it back on the bedside cabinet next to me. Softly, he unwrapped my fleecy covering, before trailing his fingers lightly over my aroused body. We made love slowly and passionately, relishing the warmth, needs and togetherness of each other's bodies. After, we laid in each other's arms, our sensual lovemaking clearing the path for a content night's slumber.

I was woken abruptly from my unconsciousness with a start. I thought I had heard a bang of some sort. Listening intently, I inconspicuously hoisted the covers protectively over me; the stairs creaked as they always seemed to do in the cranky old ancient cottage. Silence prevailed; I continued to listen, really not wanting to hear anything further. Mark stirred and sighed heavily. *Should I wake him?* I questioned my inner self. I replied, *No*, as momentarily my thoughts bickered between their selves.

The hours passed monotonously with me tossing, turning and watching the tedious luminous hand go round the clockface.

The welcome sound of the birds singing and twittering, embracing the start of a new day came as a small window of relief. I lay motionless listening to their different calls and chattering whilst the light began to sneakily invade the privacy of our bedroom.

Eventually and after much effort, I decided to get up. Exhausted, irritable and thoroughly wretched, I wearily dragged myself out of what should have been my comfortable, lovely and serene bed.

The cold hallway beckoned and so did the top conspicuously open bedroom door. I froze in my shell-shocked, zombie-like state. Staring in disbelief at the offending door for a few moments, I started to walk towards it. Halfway along the cold wooden hallway, I paused. I felt an absurd pull towards the smallest of the three bedrooms located on the left, just before the bathroom.

My eyes were instantly drawn to the single bed. I found myself gasping in shock, shuddering; the hair on the back of my neck stood up like the bristles of a brush. I stood motionless in the doorway of the room. The bed was clearly unmade, the covers blatantly pulled back like someone had just got out of it. The pillow had an obvious dent where someone's head had undoubtedly lain.

At that point I felt sheer alarm and utter terror. Someone had been in the house last night that would explain the bang and the creak on the stairwell.

I ran and violently shook my husband. "Mark! Mark! Wakeup!" I cried. "Someone has broken into our house. I heard a bang during the night, and this morning the top bedroom door is open and the bed in the little room is unmade. An intruder has definitely been here." I was trembling uncontrollably as the words came tumbling out.

"It's okay, calm down; let me take a look!" Mark swiftly threw his dressing gown on. I followed him into the hallway.

"Look, see, the covers are messy. The beds in the spare rooms haven't been touched since we made them on the second day here." I pointed frantically at the dishevelled bed linen.

Mark remained silent as he looked around the room, peering hesitantly under the bed and opening the small wooden wardrobe. I shuddered as I followed him to the top bedroom and its hateful intruding open door.

"Every morning this door is open, when at night, it is always shut!" I anxiously continued as the cold air exhaled from my mouth.

Tentatively and in excruciating silence, Mark examined the cold, bleak room. He searched under the bed, behind the dressing table and in the depths of the wardrobe. There was nothing. I followed him cautiously down the staircase. From the bottom step, I watched him search the area from top to bottom, not wanting to leave his side. We ventured into each ground-floor room until our investigation had been completed. The doors and windows were all secure and had categorically not shown any signs of being tampered with.

One further thing caught my suspicious eye, which I decided to keep to myself: my tan leather handbag which I had left in the same spot on the sofa as the previous night was once again on the floor.

CHAPTER SEVEN

We sat at our sweet-shop window, where we just sipped our hot drinks, neither of us had much of an appetite for any breakfast. The strange abnormal goings on had completely unsettled me.

"Maybe a cat found its way in when we opened one of the doors?" Mark announced satisfyingly.

"I didn't see any cats; and anyway, how could a cat be strong enough to push open that bloody top bedroom persistent door?" I argued defiantly.

"Cats can be quite clever, Ann. It's just a theory, that's all," Mark replied despondently.

"I think we should check the loft hatch; we haven't looked up there." The loft space had just sprung to my mind.

"Actually, that's a good idea. It was on our list, so let's get on with it straight away, then later we will make some calls to the building firms and get this work done." Mark cleared the mugs away and removed the stepladders and a torch from the storage cupboard in the kitchen. "Come on, you need to hold the steps for me," he said, making his way up the creaky staircase.

I duly followed, feeling like a loyal dog at its beloved owner's side. Standing rigidly at the base of the wobbly ladders, Mark edged his way carefully up each of the silver steps. At the top he pushed at the loft hatch which stubbornly remained wedged in place. Again, he thrust hard, the ladders and me both shaking at every movement. With a determined final shove, the obstinate piece of wood gave way together with a Chernobyl-like cloud of dust which gave a full layer on our unsuspecting heads and shoulders.

"Urgh! Yuck!" We both spluttered, shaking our bodies in disgust.

Mark then proceeded to offload his excess baggage on me. I quickly brushed the filth away, not even wanting to contemplate about the possibility that there could have been spiders involved.

Sub-zero artic air seemed to pour out from the square loft hatch. I handed Mark the heavy flashlight which he immediately switched on. Shining it directly upwards, he proceeded to climb into the cold, unwelcoming loft space.

"Be careful, Mark." Again, like a dog following its owner, I slowly and hesitantly climbed the steps behind him. "What's up there?" I enquired impatiently.

"A few boxes and a couple of old chests. They must have been up here for years; they are thick with dust," he replied.

I peered with eyes squinted into the eerie darkness, the iridescent flashlight beam darting quickly over the hidden treasure troves. Mark sensibly stepped onto the limited boarded areas of the icy loft space, not willing to cause a ceiling collapse.

With me barking orders from the top of the hole, we explored the unknown, the stream of light vigilantly leaving no nook or cranny unturned.

Mark somehow managed to manoeuvre the heavy boxes and ancient chests over to the hatch. "I think we should bring them down and have a better look."

I excitedly agreed.

It was a painstaking; long struggle attempting to force and wedge the secret stash down the far-from-appropriate stepladders. We carefully negotiated each twist and turn, Mark sweating profusely despite the frosty loft air.

Finally, the boxes and chests lay stacked in the hallway, seven in total. I wiped the first wooden chest down with a damp cloth. It was a handsome piece with hefty black lead straps interlocking over it. The trunk was padlocked with an old-fashioned chunk of cumbersome metal. There were two like this, and they were also the heaviest of the group.

The others, which were unlocked, contained a mix of damp, musty clothing and a few items of crockery. Pushing the crockery momentarily to one side, I continued to wipe down the intriguing chests.

Mark had gone downstairs to locate something to break open the locks. Glancing upwards, I fleetingly thought that I caught a glimpse of a small shadow in the top still-open bedroom. I carried on hearing the comforting and familiar thud of my husband's footsteps climbing the stairs.

"Mark, check the top bedroom. I swear I just saw something there." I spoke calmly and nodded towards the enemy room.

"What did you see?" he asked, sighing heavily whilst making his way towards the offending room, a pair of pliers in hand.

"It was a shadow, just briefly," I replied, as he disappeared temporarily.

"There is absolutely nothing here, Ann, just your imagination playing tricks on you. Now let's open our treasure." He frustratedly returned, eagerly clamping the teeth of the pliers around the first of the locks.

In determined silence, Mark twisted and pulled at the warped lock. Painstakingly, he began to grind away at the archaic bowed piece. Eventually and under duress, the obstinate bit of metal gave up its battle and with a chink fell to the ground. Slowly and with a struggle, Mark prised open the heavy lid and we both peered cautiously inside.

The musty, deep-rooted odour of oldness filled the air. On one side of the chest, lay piles of fragile sepia photographs depicting what seemed like the Victorian era: women dressed in elaborate long gowns, miniscule waistlines tightly pinched in and hairstyles dripping cascades of ringlets, framing their pale faces, and the gentlemen, wearing starched top hats and tails sporting grotesquely angular beards.

Packed methodically to the adjacent side was an authentic box-style camera, its bellows concertinaed into a neat, compact shape, a heavy velvety drape wrapped precisely around it.

Alongside, a doll lay forlornly, wearing a silk-trimmed gown edged with delicate lace and muslin, cotton-lined bodice with layers of exquisite petticoats. Black laced-up boots and cream stockings covered the legs and feet, with a golden locket finishing off the intricate look.

An elaborately designed silver cigarette case wrapped precisely in a cloth was pressed into the corner. In another, a silver chain with a complicated embellished magnifying glass lay meticulously neat.

"Wow, this is really interesting," I said as I attentively replaced each of the antique items.

"Might be worth something," Mark replied whilst examining a pair of what looked like operatic binoculars.

"Open the other one," I requested impatiently, trying to push the first to one side.

The stairwell creaked suddenly, and we both stared at each other. Mark swiftly stood up and looked down the staircase. Shaking his head in an uninterested fashion, he crouched next to the second unopened chest. Taking hold of the pliers, he began to tackle the protecting lock binding the secrets within. After an eternity, it finally gave up its defence, and pushing it open, we paused as we peered in.

Folds of heavy cream taffeta and gold lace met with our inquisitive eyes. A worn, small, velvet trinket box lay on top. I released it from the folds of shielding material and apprehensively opened it up. A dainty antique wedding ring intricately decorated with swirls and diamonds revealed itself to us.

I gently prised it from the box, and took a closer look; it was so tiny, almost childlike in size. I slid it tenderly onto my little finger only just managing to fit.

"It's beautiful and so delicate," I barely whispered. I took it off and handed it to Mark to inspect a little closer.

I stood up and pulled the fragile material from its hiding place. It was a magnificent wedding dress, tiny in size, a miniature boned corset in a V shape pointing down into the vast bellows of skirt. Enormous puffy shoulders morphing into slim lacy sleeves. The overall dimensions of the striking dress were astounding. It was absolutely miniscule, probably fitting the body of a ten-year-old and a very small one at that.

We both commented on its childlike proportions. It looked almost certainly of the Victorian era which again would explain the images and fashion in the numerous photographs from the first chest.

"What a find!" I exclaimed. "Goodness knows how long it's been up there."

I nodded towards the icy hole in the ceiling, surprised that icicles hadn't made a formation; it was that cold.

"I think we should do some investigating, see what we can find out," Mark said, closing the lid of the first chest. "Let's move them into the top bedroom for now."

I returned the delicate dress to its resting place, and together we dragged the boxes up the hallway to the spare room.

We decided to walk into the village to make a few enquiries for recommended contractors. Pulling on our warm jackets and scarves, we locked the doors behind us.

For once I declined the urge to look upwards at our bedroom window. I really didn't want to.

The weather had turned surprisingly colder, and I pushed my hands deep into my pockets as the bitter wind nipped expertly around my ears. We walked along the narrow pavement in subdued silence, both deep in thought and with nothing much to say.

The tiny village post office which doubles as a convenience store had a notice board advertising all manner of things with most of the local tradesmen promoting their varied skills and services. We quickly scribbled a couple of the more professional-looking ones down and enquired with several shopkeepers as to ones they themselves would recommend.

As we sipped on a cup of strong coffee at the café, Mark called the numbers, efficiently arranging to meet the various workman at staggered intervals during the course of the afternoon. We ordered a toasted cheese and ham sandwich each and discussed once again our ideas and aspirations for our new home.

My telephone interrupted us by vibrating intensely through my handbag which was draped over my chair.

"Hello, love," I answered warmly and with affection.

"Hi, Mum, how are you?" Jennifer's excited voice rattled loudly down the line.

"All good, thanks, Jen; we have settled in nicely. Meeting a few contractors later today with a view of, hopefully, starting to do some work on the place." I paused. "How are you? Are you missing not having us around the corner?" I laughed, lightheartedly.

"Yes, it's so weird, Mum," Jennifer replied wistfully.

"Aww," I sighed somewhat sadly.

"Anyway, I'm calling because we are coming down. Eve is back from Cyprus at the end of the week, so we thought we'd come and spend the weekend with you," she continued eagerly.

"That's fantastic!" I replied happily.

"Oh, and we are bringing George too."

"Wow, how fabulous!" I exclaimed. "What lovely news."

"See you on Saturday, Mum; love you."

We ended our brief conversation, and I quickly relayed what had been discussed to Mark, who was absolutely elated that the girls would be bringing his son too.

Mark's nineteen-year-old son was away at university, where he was studying for a degree in business. A keen and talented sportsman, he also participated in a vast number of extracurricular activities. Over the years, Mark had his boy strictly every other weekend, and as many other times as were allowed during his set agreed dates that had been put in place by the divorce courts.

Now that George had independently left to pursue his studies, the important decision for us to move had been a much easier one. It was a lovely surprise that all our children would be visiting on Saturday.

We quickly paid the bill and strolled up to the hotel where we made a reservation for five on Saturday night. Making our way back down the uneven cobblestones, we headed home to meet the first of the local tradesmen.

On arriving back, I felt the uneasy pull of gravity and my eyes were dragged upwards, completely and absurdly out of my control. There it was again, the net curtain pulled to one side.

I pushed the irritating sight and uneasy thoughts back to the eternal depths of my mind, finding myself struggling crossly as we opened the outer door. The unsettling thoughts rapidly returning as the patter of tiny footsteps swiftly scampered menacingly off. I glanced sideways at Mark who annoyingly once again seemed oblivious to the blatant trespassing of our home.

No sooner had we stepped over the threshold than there followed a knock on the door, and in walked the decorator who, as we were to quickly discover, was a man of very few words. However, he knew his trade, and at a pleasantly low cost, we keenly employed his services.

He was to whitewash the tired stone walls throughout the cottage, varnish the upstairs wooden floorboards and bannisters before then commencing work on the dirty decor of the greying exterior. The good news was that he was available for an immediate start, and so off he went promptly to purchase the required materials needed for his launch first thing the following morning.

On his exit, the next contractor arrived punctually. We explained our needy requirements to the easygoing builder named Mick who, whilst listening intently and asking countless questions, managed to measure and scribble vast pages of notes.

He informed us that any work that he wasn't able to do himself would be sub-contracted out to his reliable sources. He seemed extremely pleasant and thorough. He knew of the cottage as he had lived locally for his entire life, remarking that it would be nice to see it lived in again after being empty for so long. I found myself liking him and his pleasant attitude which turned out to be a godsend as the other contractor failed to even show up.

Mick left us after two hours, sincerely promising to return the next day with his estimates and ideas. He also was available for an immediate start, saying that work locally nowadays was difficult to come by.

"He seemed a nice enough chap," Mark said as he firmly closed the door.

"Yes, I liked him; he seemed really genuine," I replied, kicking off my shoes. "Let's see what he has to say tomorrow."

CHAPTER EIGHT

The alarm woke me abruptly at seven. The room seemed intensely dark, with no bright lights seeping through the gaps in the curtains. I could hear the sound of rain beating heavily down on the windows, the splashes of the drops landing in the ever-increasing puddles down on the pavement below, making me want to snuggle down into the sheets even further. I stretched and left the security and bliss of my wonderful bed.

I knew immediately that the door would be open in the top bedroom. Once again, I was right. There it was fully ajar and wedged solid on the uneven, warped floorboards. I exhaled heavily. Ironically, I had almost come to expect it. The strange thing was this morning it didn't seem to bother me. Tonight, I would leave it open as a reverse tactic, I defiantly and rebelliously thought.

I paused momentarily as I reached the doorway of the smallest bedroom; my stomach fluttered as I nervously peered in. There was, thankfully, nothing out of place. Was this going to become my routine every morning, I wondered cynically.

Gerry, the silent decorator, arrived promptly not long after, his faded white overalls splattered with various shades of paint. We agreed he would start in the back lounge and work his way through. This would be subject to change once we had organised the works to commence. I exasperatedly picked up my bag from its discarded position on the floor to make way for the onslaught of dustsheets which would protect the walkway to the lounge. As I did so, I observed a small shadow glide fleetingly up the stairs. Mark and Gerry were talking in the lounge; I could hear the muffled echo of their voices.

As the translucent shadow vanished almost as quickly as it had appeared, I vaguely heard the sound of a child laughing. The hairs stood up on the back of my neck, a seemingly regular occurrence now, the realisation suddenly submerging, drowning and swamping me: the cottage was undeniably haunted.

I wanted to scream at the top of my voice, but what was the point? I needed to understand exactly what the uninvited presence was and, more importantly, why it hadn't 'passed over'.

My laptop lay frustratingly idle in the cottage. We were still waiting for the internet to be installed, so until this had been accomplished, I was unable to make any use of it for the research I so needed to do. I made a mental note to chase up the provider that morning.

Mark obliviously wandered back into the room. I would speak to him later once Mick the builder had returned with his estimates. In the meantime, I was going to pay a visit to our neighbours.

Making lame excuses to Mark, I hurriedly left the cottage and walked up our neighbours' immaculately lined pathway. When I reached the entrance of the bright pillar-box red front door, I rapped the knocker a little loudly and probably somewhat impatiently.

"Good morning, Freida," I greeted warmly. "Have you a few minutes to spare me?"

"Hello, Ann, of course, we have. Come on inside and have a cup of tea," she replied as I followed her hastily.

Albert welcomed me into their quaint kitchen where he gestured me to take a seat at the small dining table covered in a red checked, gingham-like tablecloth. I stared blankly around the room. It was cluttered in a nice, homely way with heaving shelving filled with an abundance of pots and pans; an overly stocked larder of which the contents, when Freida had opened the door, had almost tumbled out over her; and yellow-painted cupboards snaking around the kitchen walls, lined in a garishly fussy wallpaper.

Freida placed a teapot wearing a comical, hand-knitted half tea cosy onto the table, accompanied by pretty, gold-rimmed porcelain teacups decorated in crimson roses, which looked almost too delicate and fragile to drink from.

"How are you settling on, pet?" she asked as she expertly poured weak tea into each of the flowery cups. "Care for some milk?"

"Yes, please," I answered. "Yes, it's all going well, thanks. We have the decorator starting today." I hesitated. "Erm... there are just a couple of things I wanted to ask you, if you don't mind?" I paused for a moment, not really knowing how to position my question. "Have you heard anything strange about the cottage?"

I waited, patiently watching for their reactions if any. I was certain that I noticed Albert briefly glance uncomfortably in the direction of his wife.

"What do you mean strange, pet?" came the somewhat disappointing reply.

"I'm not entirely sure." I briefly paused. "Just, a few things have happened which are a little bit peculiar, and I can't really find an explanation for them." I found myself sighing wearily, thinking subconsciously that this conversation was going absolutely nowhere.

I continued, "I thought you might have been able to help me understand; that's all really." I looked towards Freida's face in the faint glimmer of hope that the indifferent look she was displaying might change.

"We haven't heard of any strange goings on, have we, Albert?" She didn't let her husband reply. "No, nothing at all." With that she changed the subject brusquely. "Miserable weather today, isn't it?"

I left soon after, having accomplished the square route of zero. As I walked dejectedly away from their home, the sound of raised voices reached my ears.

CHAPTER NINE

I stepped carefully over the dust sheets, the overwhelming smell of paint fumes engulfing the normally musty air. Mark was standing in the kitchen with Mick the builder making tea. The timing was perfect as I momentarily put the disturbed thoughts whirling inside my head to one side.

"Mick has brought the estimate. We were just about to go through his ideas!" Mark handed over the mugs filled with strong tea. I took one to Gerry who seemed to be totally transfixed in his own little world of pungent fumes and paint. He was probably high in the haze of emulsion.

I joined the two men at our sweet-shop table, and we went through with a fine-tooth comb every aspect of the planned works. We also agreed, unitedly, that we would replace the old kitchen. This would mean it far more cost-effective in the long term rather than completing it over a staggered and prolonged period of time. Primarily, more than anything, I wanted to cleanse this little cottage, expel its past and remove this ghostly presence that was invading it; maybe that was what was needed? I questioned my inner self contentiously as Mick worked out the efficient plan of action.

Whilst they painstakingly continued to go over valid points and suggestions, I called the internet provider. Irritated, I muttered at the bored 'heard-it-all-before' voice on the other end of the line at having to call a premium number only to be put on hold for an eternity before I received a reply, coupled with the fact of the sheer inconvenience caused. I could have gone on and on venting my frustrations, but I needed the internet. Eventually, I managed to obtain a cancellation spot, and it was booked in for the following day. I retreated satisfied that I had won my battle.

Mick once again methodically measured the kitchen and bathroom. He left us with piles of brochures containing extensive ranges and images, leaving us to the decision of which one. An enhanced, computerised 3D design had provided our chosen final layout, so that we could picture the final result.

He was a likeable guy, and both he and Gerry had crossed paths numerous times before in the working environment, which was another bonus. He was to return tomorrow, which was Friday, to start the basic groundwork; although we had requested that nothing overly drastic was to commence until the Monday when the children would be long gone.

I took the opportunity to say to Mark that we needed to chat. I had to tell him about the creepy shadows, my mysteriously agile bag and the over-dishevelled moving curtain, all of which I hadn't mentioned before.

We decided to have dinner at the hotel again, the overpowering nauseous paint fumes pushing us directly on that path. It was an easy decision; they also had internet access which for me, at this point in time, was an urgent requirement. I arranged to meet Mark there, as he had a few minor jobs around the cottage, explaining nonchalantly that I had emails that needed attending to.

This time I wasn't going to look up as I closed the front door behind me. I felt the strong magnetic pull coming from the direction of the window. I ignored it, painstakingly gripping my bag firmly, together with the laptop. I felt almost childlike with my disobedience. My head and eyes ached trying to withstand the wrenching and power that the window seemingly had over me.

I walked slowly and boldly, each step taking me further away from the reach and clasp of its hypnotic panes. Focusing, I crossed the road, embracing my freedom, becoming increasingly stronger with each ongoing pace.

A straggly black cat suddenly ran in front of me, darting quickly across the road to where I had just come from. Momentarily distracted, my eyes followed it then weakened foolishly as they were grasped into the seduction of the window. I knew what I would see; I had almost resigned myself to the painfully obvious.

There it was, as I had expected, a small white face peering out between the slim gap in the net curtains. Petite and innocent-looking in appearance, a translucent, forlorn, childlike manifestation.

I stared calmly, not wanting to lose the haunting image before me. It was still and void of emotion. Eerily, it continued to stare, motionless, with sad vacant eyes, dark pool-like hollows.

Fleetingly, my eyes diverted to the right. I saw Freida's thin, wiry face peering from behind her twitching curtain. I quickly returned my gaze towards the window; the pale, haunting figure had vanished. Glimpsing back at our neighbours' window, it came as no surprise that Freida had also gone.

Disturbed, I continued up to the hotel and arrived, having taken in absolutely nothing of my walk. Our snug little table was free; however, I chose one of the huge leather armchairs directly in front of the glowing embers. Commandeering my place, I pulled my laptop impatiently from my bag. It connected effortlessly to the hotel wi-fi. I quickly started typing in words associated with the village: old village sweet shop, ghosts, murders and castle. A few sightings were repeated time and time again, the castle featuring predominately among those.

The sightings included a mysterious grey lady appearing eerily in the shadows of corridors; a foot guard wearing a strange three-pointed hat which manifested in blurry shapes of faces; a man in green, apparently, frequently spotted wandering through the castle gift shop which used to form part of the old stable block, and items in the shop would inexplicably tumble and an odd sticky brown substance would coat the goods.

I continued to browse. 'In July 1951, a group of visiting tourists heard a number of marching people approaching their location. The noise was so loud and unbearable that they had ran in terror, apparently not stopping until they had reached the base of the hill.'

Another headline: 'In a large goods shed in the village station, a man was killed in a freak accident. He is now reported to haunt the location of his death, his shadowy form unnerving people.'

I read on: 'In September 1964, within the old nunnery, a 14th-century building which was once incorporated into the nearby monastic buildings and thought originally to be used as a guesthouse for the priory had another story to tell. An old report stated that a witness awoke suddenly to find a figure wearing flowing robes and standing motionless at the base of her bed. She had screamed hysterically, and the figure supposedly melted rapidly away; her cries woke her husband who didn't see a thing.'

As interesting as these sightings were, nothing was shedding any light on the one haunting that I needed to find an explanation for. My painstaking search was proving to be to no avail. I looked at my watch. It was nearly six o'clock; Mark would be arriving shortly. Ordering myself a glass of wine, I sat sipping it as my efforts continued.

The hotel, I discovered whilst searching, also had a fascinatingly colourful past dating back to the 16th century where it was originally a coaching hostelry. Evidently, it played a significant role in the Civil War where it housed Colonel Blake's roundheads during its harrowing 160-day siege of the then Royalist-held castle.

Engrossed in my unproductive research, I failed to notice Mark taking a seat in the chair opposite. He laughed as I ignored the strange presence adjacent to me.

"Oh, hello!" I said smiling when I eventually looked up.

"You look thoroughly absorbed in your work!" he said laughing, as I closed the lid firmly on the laptop.

"Yes, I have been; I didn't realise the time, to be honest." I sipped my wine. "I have been trying to find out the history of the village and, more importantly" – I paused – "our cottage."

"You think it's haunted, don't you?" Mark replied instantly and catching me completely off guard.

"I don't think, Mark, I know it definitely is, and there are a few things that I haven't told you!"

"Like what?" he questioned.

"I saw a face, a childlike being at our bedroom window as I left today. The curtain in that room seems to move out of place every day!" I hesitated, waiting for Mark's reaction. He was listening intently as I continued, "My handbag, which I leave in the same place on the sofa under the stairs every night is on the floor in the morning. Oh, and I keep seeing shadow-like figures out of the corner of my eye." I stopped, wilfully waiting for a response.

"Okay..." Mark now paused thoughtfully. "I need to now tell you something."

"What?" I found myself gasping.

"Last night, in bed, I woke up suddenly. I opened my eyes and..." He gulped sharply before inhaling a deep intake of breath. He carried on, "I looked in the direction of the doorway, and I saw a small child standing there; just staring at me, motionless! I kept trying to blink to make it disappear, also thinking that it was maybe a dream, but it didn't."

It was Mark's turn to now wait for my reaction.

"Oh my God, why didn't you wake me?" I stammered.

"I really didn't want to worry you. I know that you had been hearing the children's voices and footsteps." He paused again momentarily. "It was just standing there, staring at me with big, round, sad eyes."

"Was it a boy or girl? How old do you think it was?" I questioned, still fairly shocked.

"That's the weird thing, Ann; I couldn't tell the gender. It was about this high." He motioned his arm upwards demonstrating the height of a small child. He continued, "It had blond curls almost like ringlets, and it was wearing an old-fashioned white bed shirt. It could have been either." Mark rubbed his forehead in a perplexed manner.

We both sat in deep silence for a few minutes, contemplating everything that each other had said.

"What shall we do?" I said, interrupting the stillness.

"Well, I really think we should try to find out more. Are you happy to stay there?" Mark raised the question I somehow sensed he'd ask.

"I think so," I replied in a calm whisper. "I didn't feel scared today when I noticed the face at the window; I felt strangely sad."

Mark nodded his head in acknowledgement. "I was the same when I saw the child in the doorway. It looked desperately sorrowful."

"Maybe it needs our help?" I said sympathetically.

"Let's see what we can find out. Maybe Freida next door can help us?" Mark responded.

"I tried that this morning, although I didn't actually ask them outright; I just enquired if they had heard of anything strange with our cottage. Without any hesitation, Freida said that they knew nothing!" I said shaking my head unconvincingly.

"I think we need to find out who has lived at the cottage firstly, find out the family tree, and then make enquiries from there." Mark took a deep breath before continuing. "We have a huge pile of photographs in that chest we brought down from the loft. We might find some answers in those."

We chinked glasses in mutual agreement, Mark seemingly pleased with his clever suggestion.

We ordered another drink as we browsed through the now familiar menu. It was becoming a second home for us the number of times we had been in there. We both decided on the haddock and leek fishcakes which were served with a dressed mixed leaf salad. They were delicious and went down very nicely.

We discussed the day's events once again, and Mark updated me on the progress of Gerry the silent decorator, who had apparently achieved quite a lot in just one day, obviously to do with the fact that he rarely spoke, clearly preferring the solitude of his sombre hush enveloping him.

Mick had also phoned, as promised. The boiler and its antiquated heating system would thankfully be replaced on Monday, and he suggested thoughtfully that it might be a good idea if we were to make ourselves scarce for the day, so as to avoid all the disruption. We decided that we would use the opportunity to drive into town where we would be able to spend a few hours in the mammoth library. There we would hopefully be able to piece together the secret past of the cottage.

We also agreed not to mention any of our ghostly happenings to the children when they arrived on Saturday. However, it had crossed my mind that they were staying overnight, and inwardly, I prayed that our little 'friend' behaved and stayed well out of sight.

We left the hotel at around nine. It had been a nice evening spent together, and I felt relieved that we had shared our strange experiences and unsettled feelings. We both agreed a pact that if either of us encountered any more paranormal activities, then we were to immediately inform the other.

The irregular cobblestones always seemed a bit easier to negotiate with a drink or two inside. We walked along the pretty little street until we finally reached home. Out of habit I glanced upwards towards the guilt-ridden window; surprisingly, nothing had changed from earlier.

"Listen for the children as we go in," I whispered in Mark's ear as we opened the outer door.

The smell of fresh paint immediately engulfed us as we walked through the entrance. True to form, they hurriedly scurried off laughing. It was like a game, mocking and taunting us. Nonetheless, Mark had clearly heard the faint sounds in the distance. I placed my handbag in its spot on the sofa before heading up the creaky old staircase. Faltering midway, I turned back to go down. Carefully lifting my bag from its resting place, I positioned it on the floor directly in front of the sofa, the exact same spot it appeared on in the morning. I pointed at what I was doing for Mark's benefit then raised my finger to my mouth to maintain hushed silence.

Once upstairs, I made a point of wedging the top bedroom door firmly open. Arrogantly and ever so slightly haughtily, I walked off. *Let the games commence,* I thought, almost sneering in the back of my wicked little mind.

CHAPTER TEN

Seven o'clock sharp, my alarm echoed violently around the bedroom. Mark stirred and moaned as he usually did when woken from his slumber. Surprisingly, I had slept really well, the wine the night before obviously taking its full effect. I got up immediately, excited almost to see if my reverse play strategy had accomplished any results.

My eyes instantaneously fell directly upon the conspiring door opposite, and to my minor disappointment, the obstinate door remained where I had forcibly compressed it the night before. I huffed loudly to myself, as I peered eagerly over the banister to the lounge below. I stared at my bag, the innocent player of my game. It was neatly placed upon the sofa where it should have spent the night. I smiled as I acknowledged the fact that we unquestionably had a poltergeist of sorts living under the same roof.

Gerry the silent decorator arrived at seven thirty sharp and began his laborious day's work. He had, as Mark said, progressed remarkably well, with the back lounge expertly finished. Today he was to embark upstairs, the top imposing bedroom being the first on his list.

I gathered a pile of photographs from the chest as Gerry maneuvred his smelly dust sheet around the icy room. 'Manifests itself in other ways, such as noises, chills or iridescent orbs.' I suddenly recalled an article that I had read during one of my searches yesterday. It would definitely explain the bitter Antarctic chill in this room, I thought as I closed the lid of the heavy chest.

Mick arrived half an hour later and noisily started his preparations for the following week. Over breakfast, Mark and I spent time choosing the kitchen, a light ash grey contemporary style with sleek silver handles which complimented the look. We had both decided on an old-fashioned butler sink which would only add to the existing features of the beautiful old cottage. I indulgingly and after a minor argument had chosen a jet black granite worktop with a sparkling fleck of silver.

The bathroom was an easier decision, and staying in keeping with the original style, we chose a white suite with the added luxury of a rainforest shower. It briefly crossed my mind as we made our expensive choices, would we be actually staying?

The internet provider arrived mid-morning. As expected, the cottage was a hive of activity and commotion. I noticed Freida walking by, noticeably prying in as she passed the window.

As the chaotic mayhem went on around us, Mark and I started sifting through the archaic pile of delicate sepia photographs. The powerful images portrayed a very contrasting and thought-provoking past. As we prudently studied the pictures, Mark used the magnifying glass we had found in the chest to enhance the faces and features, giving them much more clarity.

The face I had observed in the window had appeared almost opaque. I tried in vain to match it with one of the meaningless faces in the prints. I pulled a couple to one side to scrutinise a bit further when suddenly Mark gasped.

"That's it!" he exclaimed eagerly as he pushed the grainy photo in front of me.

"It's a girl; she's about six, I would say. Is this your figure in the doorway?" I asked staring intently at the image.

Pictured clearly outside the barely unchanged exterior of the cottage, the girl was dressed in a drab, dark-coloured dress with a white lacey trimmed pinafore layered over the top. Her fair jaw-length ringlets framing her wretched face, she wore a white lacy bonnet over her curls. One thing stood predominately out: the overpowering sense of sadness and haunting melancholy of the picture.

"Yes! That's it— I mean her!" Mark replied craning his neck to look more closely.

I turned over the photograph, and on the reverse were the faint markings of a pencil.

Mark held the magnifying glass to it. "I think it says 1901 or maybe 1907." Mark strained his eyes even harder. "Alice! That's her name," he declared triumphantly.

"Surname?" I questioned.

"No, nothing else."

Alice appeared in another miserable photo with someone we assumed would have been her mother; a tiny, delicate young thing, no more than a child herself. The clothing that they were wearing seemed to represent an inferior, less-fortunate class: the starched white pinafores they wore over sullen, dark unflattering dresses; the prim white bonnets covering most of their neatly trimmed, almost-identical tresses, black laced-up shoes over dark stockings. The images portrayed that there was a possibility they may have been servants.

There were no markings on the back of this photograph, but we now had another figure to trace, hopefully, leading us to further clues to unravel. It was captivating as we laid to one side our findings, trying to piece together the intricate and enthralling jigsaw.

Alice's mother appeared in several other photographs. One looked like a small family gathering, where her slight figure almost disappeared. Standing timidly in the shadows, four others stood in the forefront, outshining the meek little mouse cowering behind. Another print portrayed a very different image. She was dressed head to toe in black, a sombre shawl draped dramatically across her hair, her head hunched solemnly downwards; she looked to be desperately mourning.

The final picture showed her with a man. He towered over her miniscule frame; she was peering innocently upwards towards him, her face woeful and full of sorrow. He looked irritated and clearly harbouring a little animosity towards her. It painted yet another formidable picture. This photograph, however, appeared to have a marking on.

"William and Elisabeth Wraith 1901," Mark deciphered with the help of the magnifying glass. "Now we have another piece of the jigsaw!"

We found William Wraith in two other photographs, each one only bearing him. He stood intimidatingly in well-dressed attire unlike his sorrowful wife who seemed to be poverty stricken. We were still unsure if Elisabeth was Alice's mother, and also if the noble William was, in fact, her father. There were a few features which likened her to both of them, but the grainy images could easily play tricks on your mind, and after a while, anyone could have been the poor child's relative.

I studied carefully the couple of pictures that earlier I had pushed to one side. There was a faint possibility that they resembled the dark face which had revealed itself to me yesterday at the top window. Looking more closely at Elisabeth's sallow features, however, made me think it could well have been her.

We found other faded names and dates among the piles of images, which we wrote down in a notebook. From all the information that we had before us, there appeared to be no further links to the Wraiths or to little Alice; nonetheless, we had the corner pieces of the jigsaw.

The internet provider had completed what he had to do, and ten minutes later my laptop successfully connected to the internet. We also had multiple channels to chose from, much to Mark's instant elation.

Wasting no time at all, I hastily began to type in the names William and Elisabeth Wraith. Seconds later, social networking sites began popping up with numerous inappropriate options. I typed in the date 1901 only to have 'trace your family tree' type sites frustratingly emerging, heckling for subscribers and offering countless fourteen day 'free' trials.

I persevered and tried typing in parish registers; of which I finally obtained some useful information and, more importantly, some direction.

According to the various articles, records of civil registration were made compulsory in 1875, although some of the handwritten 18th-century entries were apparently particularly difficult to decipher. Anglican registers of baptism, marriage and burial were ordered to be kept from as early as 1538.

Another easily traceable area that was available for public viewing was the census returns. These were taken every ten years from 1801, although actual names were not included until 1841. It was also indicated that the earlier censuses were not informative; relationships between those living in each household were not stated and ages over fifteen were rounded down to the nearest multiples of five.

However, in 1851 this changed as all the information was supplied. I clicked on a few of the helpful links and found out that the Bristol Central Reference Library held censuses for eighty parishes in Somerset covering the period of 1841 to 1891. This should cover the exact information that we were looking for. I quickly wrote the contacts down.

I tapped 'newspapers in 1900', and a couple of pages came up. I clicked on *Western Gazette*. It covered most parts of Somerset from 1863 to 1970 with the most newsworthy events such as accidents, murders, deaths and marriages taking a much higher precedence over the more mundane incidents. This information I discovered was held on microfilms at the local history library. Again, I scribbled these details down in my increasingly busy notebook. Monday was going to be quite an exciting day, but at the same time, I felt slightly apprehensive at what we would discover.

I walked into the kitchen and put the kettle on. I had been lost in thought and my research, almost oblivious to the chaotic noise going on around me. Mark followed me in, and handing him a cup of coffee, I summarised briefly what I had been able to find out. He acknowledged by patting me on the back in an affectionate manner. I felt like a school kid having completed its homework.

Returning to my haven in the sweet-shop window, I placed my cup down on the table and noticed a couple of the photographs lying face down on the floor under the table. Reaching beneath, I dragged them back towards me, somehow managing to scrape them up with my lack of manicured nails and a stupidly awkward position.

I looked at the prints. They were the two of William arrogantly posing, solely on his own in all his grandeur. They hadn't blown off the table by accident. There was no breeze, doors or windows open, and the position they were in would have been totally impossible to have fallen down to. These photos had purposely been placed there, in the short space of time I had taken walking to the kitchen, making us a coffee and returning back again.

I stared bluntly at William's egotistical stance. He looked full of conceited self-importance, his dark eyes peering back at me in a creepy condescending manner. I shuddered visibly, deciding there and then that I didn't really care much for him. Harshly and somewhat scornfully, I threw the pictures to one side, discarding them in a repulsed fashion.

At that precise point, a child's muffled laugh followed by a faint, almost unclear, "Sshh!" echoed gently down the stairwell. I glanced up instantly to the direction of where the noise had originated. There, fleetingly, the small evanescent dark shadow that I briefly caught sight of vanished into thin air.

As I stared vacantly into the space where our little friend had been, thoughts flooded around my already overworked mind. She had found that amusing, me discarding the photographs in that revolted way.

I stared back at William's narcissistic face then momentarily back at the stairwell, picking up the two photos, I threw them down as I had before, expressing my disgust in an over-the-top theatrical way.

Listening intently, I heard the faintest child's laughter, and as I returned my gaze towards the top of the stairs, there was a tiny shadow peering down at me, a small girl's head.

That was the exact reaction that I had hoped for. I scooped up the photos again and repeatedly threw them down on the floor. Turning round to stare at the little head, I waited for any response. A tiny, almost inaudible giggle followed, and then my apparition disappeared as clumsy, heavy footsteps pounded along the upstairs hallway.

Gerry the silent decorator decided at that moment in time to surface from his noiseless world and for once not be so quiet. I huffed overly loudly, irate to say the least.

Over dinner, and once again by ourselves, other than the manifesting dwelling with us, I told Mark every single detail of my encounter with Alice. I decided that we should now call her that and tried demonstrating the photo trick to him, unsurprisingly to no avail. My ghostly friend was definitely having none of it and was certainly not going to perform her tricks in front of my bewildered husband. I gave up, and we sat watching a scary horror film on our multi-channel TV, probably not one of the wisest choices we had ever made.

I walked, rather ran up to bed, hastily washing, cleaning my teeth and being overly careful not to look in the bathroom mirror, because seemingly that's where you always saw ghosts manifesting. I swiftly pelted to bed, covers wrapped tightly over my head. I felt safe once more, even if I was sweating profusely.

CHAPTER ELEVEN

We both got up extra early. Our children were due to arrive mid-morning, and I wanted to tidy up as much as possible. Gerry the silent decorator had fortunately finished the top bedroom where the girls would be sleeping that night. We dusted, polished and washed down all the surfaces. It smelt fresh and cleansed in there now, although an icy chill still remained unnervingly in the air.

'Manifests in chills'; the words swirled erratically around my mind as I hastily continued to clean. The bedroom looked lovely with its crisp white walls. I placed fresh, fragrant white roses bought the previous day in a glass vase on the dressing table. The bright sunshine shone through the leaded light windows, leaving patterns of light glimmering on the floor. I slowly stared around; it looked beautiful.

The girls would have to share the double bed which was more than adequate in size for them both. George would be staying in the smallest bedroom, which we had also cleaned thoroughly of all the dust particles which had somehow managed to find their way in. I laid out fresh towels in both rooms and put a sentimental cuddly toy on each of their pillows, something I had always done despite their now adult years. I could hear Mark mopping the floors vigorously downstairs whilst singing loudly and

82

appallingly out of tune. He was obviously wearing his headphones.

The sound of Eve's Mini Cooper roared down the road, momentarily breaking the silence of the village; both girls had purchased identical cars with their inheritance. I looked out of the window and could see their smiling faces as they pulled round onto the driveway. George sat sullenly in the back, probably fed up with listening to their relentless girly nattering on the journey down. I ran out of the door to greet them.

"Hello," I said giving Eve a huge hug as she emerged stiffly from her long drive.

"Hi, Mum," she replied returning my hug twice as hard. Jennifer stepped from the car, sliding the seat forward so that George was able to clamber out.

"Hello, you two." I reached my arms out to cuddle my other children.

Mark came running out to greet the clan.

Jennifer leaned inside the car and lifted out a furry wide-eyed bundle, handing it to me with excitement in her eyes. "This is Fred, a present for you both." She offloaded the tiny little creature with a smile.

"Oh, isn't he cute?" I shrieked loudly. "He is absolutely adorable!" I stared down at the little innocent face looking back at me. Fred was a French bulldog puppy, and he was utterly gorgeous: little legs, bug-like adoring eyes and ears that were ginormous in comparison to his chubby little body. He licked my chin in appreciation.

"Look at him!" I pushed Fred up towards Mark's impassive face; he turned his nose up in slight disgust as he wasn't really a dog lover. Fred showed his gratitude by weeing in an upward fashion all over my husband's branded sweater, a hard golden shower aimed swiftly and competently in the appropriate direction.

"Urgh!" was the mortified response that followed. Mark was not in the least bit amused, his jumper now displaying a rather large and smelly damp patch, courtesy of the alien-lookalike dog. I winked at the girls and smiled to myself as I carried my little pooch to his new home.

The five of us sauntered through the doors. The children had on various occasions visited the cottage before our move down as we had wanted to seek their prior approval. Their favourable gazes as they looked around only added to the fact that they were in agreement that we had done the right thing.

Fred wandered in and out of the downstairs rooms, looking lost in the wilderness of the old stone floors. Jennifer positioned an oversized furry bed which she had purchased for him, on the large bottom step of the stairwell, and he managed surprisingly to scramble up and plonk himself clumsily in, barking as he did so in self-satisfaction.

We sat down, slightly squashed at the sweet-shop window. I prepared a hearty full breakfast followed by numerous rounds of toast and jam which the children devoured almost instantly. Each updated us on their news, and before we knew it, a couple of hours had passed quickly by, with us listening and chatting constantly.

I turned to look at our new little addition; he remained utterly exhausted, still laying in his huge, encompassing comfy bed, cute little snores escaping every so often from his squashed, screwed-up face. Every now and then, he would manage to open his huge grey eyes and look adoringly up towards us before finding it far too tiring, his head then collapsing once more into the comfy padding of his sumptuous bed.

I stood up and began to clear the table whilst the unceasing chatter continued. Up Fred unsteadily clambered and tumbled down the bottom step to follow, stumbling yet again as he violently shook his little body in an effort to wake himself up. He chased me haphazardly into the kitchen, deciding unforgivingly to wee erratically all the way. I chastised my naive pup, picking him promptly up and placing him on the wee pad we had put down at the back door. I daftly explained in a human-like way that in future that's where he needed to go. He just looked at me with adorable, loving eyes; he was the cutest puppy I had ever seen.

I opened the back door, and Fred cautiously and nervously followed. I clipped his blue lead on to his matching little blue harness which the girls had also thoughtfully bought along with an abundance of food items and toys. Carefully, I scrutinised our small courtyard garden for any holes or areas of potential escape routes. I spotted a small gap towards the rear, immediately blocking it off with a large heavy stone. Now the courtyard had become a secure and totally invincible fortress for our new little man to take full advantage of.

Now that he was unable to escape, I took off his lead, and he bounced happily around like a spring lamb. I washed the dishes whilst watching him chase then run away from the autumnal leaves, playing a game of tag, barking and trying to eat them as they caught up with him.

Jennifer came into the kitchen and gave me a hug. "Do you like him, Mum?" she asked, whilst amusingly peering out at Fred over the stable door into the garden below.

"I do. He is perfect, and it will be lovely to have him here. There are so many nice places to walk with him. I think I may have some work to do with Mark though," I said, smiling at the cheeky bundle of fun outside.

We had earlier decided to take the children into the town. It had more to offer in the way of vibrant life than the quiet serenity that our village could provide. We thought it would be best to shut Fred in the kitchen where damage would be far more limited. He seemed quite content settling once more into the comfort of his cozy bed, his little body clearly worn out from his frivolous activities.

Mark slowly drove the scenic route out so that everyone could fully appreciate the beautifully picturesque surroundings, pointing at all the interesting landmarks along the way. We parked in the busy pay and display car park situated on the gusty sea front.

Saturdays were always a hub of excitement in town as a lively bustling market took place weekly, a popular choice with the locals who left with bags fully laden with fresh produce and bargain bucket buys.

The five of us spent an hour meandering around the blowing stalls. I picked up some fresh fruit and vegetables, together with an extra-large chicken for the roast dinner I had planned to cook the next day. Both girls happily chose bright fake designer bags which to their delight I treated them to. Mark bought himself a couple of lambswool jumpers, and George picked up a cool cover for his expensive smartphone which he barely seemed to put down.

We put our highly extravagant purchases in the boot of the car before heading into the town centre, stopping at the amusement arcade on the way. The deafeningly noisy vibrating machines occupied everyone for another hour, and we came away with armfuls of cheap silly toys which we had surprisingly and skilfully managed to win on the extortionate claw-like grabbers. We could have easily paid the exact same amount in a shop and would have come away with a far more superior item. However, the spellbinding experience had by all, clearly wouldn't have had the same effect.

Another hour was spent venturing in and out of the various range of shops. The girls disappeared off for a while as the call of the little unique boutiques reached out to them.

Having thoroughly exhausted Mark's patience threshold with shopping, we decided welcomingly, to pause for a coffee break and stopped at our favourite little pavement café. We ordered hot drinks as we sat chatting in the busy surroundings.

A short while later, my spendthrift daughters returned, arms heavily laden with shopping bags. They pulled out various items, patiently waiting for my seal of approval, both ordering hot chocolates topped with a mountain of indulgent whipped cream and marshmallows at the same time. Mark organised refills for us, and we chatted more, making the most of the precious time being spent with our children.

Finishing our fulfilling hot drinks, we headed back towards the seafront, where we strolled up towards the vibrant hues of the beach huts. Pausing, for a few moments, we took in the vast magnitude and power of the angry unforgiving sea: towering, uncontrollable waves showing absolutely no remorse as they battered the innocent beach and the Jurassic-like cliffs, the wind tearing into them, whipping the water into a wildly savage frenzy.

It was a mesmerising and hypnotic sight, the sea showing no repentance whilst commanding the deepest of respect. We watched in admiration for a while before making our way back, the sharp autumn wind now blowing a gale. My hair harshly thrashing my now rosy cheeks, my ears tingling with cold and my eyes streaming, we struggled to walk against the abusive torrent. The sea, meanwhile, continuing to offend its guiltless shoreline alongside us.

For just a short period of time, I had forgotten about poor little Alice and the Wraiths. I momentarily pictured baby Fred, instantly wondering how he was. *Did animals have a sixth sense?* I asked myself suddenly. My two inner selves finding no excuse to actively begin arguing the fact, eventually and after much conflict and debate, it was agreed that they most certainly did.

A little tired after our altercation with the gale, we arrived back at the car. We had a couple of hours to spare before our table reservation at the hotel. Mark drove us home, and we unloaded the shopping. I inconspicuously made a point of listening as we entered the cottage. The faint footsteps scurried off in the distance as I had expected that they would do. No one else seemed to hear; it had just been for the benefit of my own keen ears.

I opened the kitchen door gently. Two huge, bewildered eyes slowly opened, and within seconds, Fred bumbled clumsily from his slumber to greet me, weeing once more in his excitement. I quickly dragged him over to the wee pad, where he managed to position himself into a more controlled toilet. Praising him in a babyish fashion, I unlocked the back door. He ran out, excitedly bounding in a gangly, Bambi-like demeanour.

I showed the children their rooms, and immediately they began arguing who would use the bathroom first.

"Mum, it's so cold in here!" Eve commented, hugging her arms around herself as I turned to leave the icy room.

"I know; I think it's because it's the rear of the cottage," I said very convincingly." I will get Mark to drag out the small convector heater; it will get rid of the chill."

I called downstairs to Mark, asking him to take out the appliance from the storage cupboard in the kitchen. Within minutes Mark appeared with the convector in hand. He plugged the saviour in, and almost instantaneously, the heat ripped through the cold air.

The well-used bathroom had a constant flow of visitors with the water, not surprisingly, running cold at my poor suffering husband's turn. I put on a simple black dress with black tights and black leather boots; I curled my freshly washed hair. It felt incredibly nice that we were dressing up for dinner. Mark commented on my appearance, flatteringly saying how beautiful I looked. I returned the compliment as we waited patiently for our children to finally appear.

I gave Fred a big cuddle before putting him back to bed. He didn't seem to mind; he had been fed, his little tummy bloated and full, done his bits; then like a newborn baby he needed his sleep. We left him holed up in his corner in the kitchen, the light left dimly on for his comfort. I quickly grabbed my camera on the way out so I could take some up-to-date photographs of one of the rare occasions we were all actually together.

"I'm starving!" George said as we locked the front door.

"Same!" Jen acknowledged, in an exaggerated weakened stance, depicting starvation.

We took a tranquil walk up the cobbled high street, stopping every now and then to meander at the imaginative window displays as we strode along. I silently thought of the haunted, woeful face in our top bedroom window that had once again revealed itself to me as we had departed.

Arriving at the imposing hotel entrance, we stopped to admire the view of the picturesque village. Prettily lit up, it looked almost fairytale like.

"It's so pretty, Mum, isn't it?" Jen exclaimed as she observed the endearing landscape laid out in front of her.

"It is, Jen; you can see why we moved here now, can't you?" I replied affectionately as everyone nodded in mutual agreement.

We stood at the bar and ordered drinks, deciding to take full advantage of the unusually vacant bar stools whilst we awaited our reservation time. I turned to look at Mark. He caught my yearning eyes, and we winked acknowledging each other in reciprocated agreement. He looked contented.

I turned my gaze towards our chattering children; it was lovely to have them visit and unexpectedly made me feel a large pang of guilt for having moved away. I hastily pushed the negative feelings from my mind and thought positively again, joining in the ever-growing animated conversation.

Politely, following a couple of drinks later, we were called to our table. Taking our allocated places, Mark ordered a bottle of the hotel's finest champagne in celebration and domineeringly chinked our uncomplaining flutes. We hungrily ordered our food with everyone having seventies-style prawn cocktail starters in funny little silver dishes. Laughing and joking, the evening went exceptionally well, and the night seemed to whisk by in a flash.

As the others ordered desserts, a clear sign of gluttony, I sat contemplating quietly, taking in the enveloping warmth of my family surrounding me; briefly invaded by surreal thoughts of our cottage and its mysterious manifestations. Hopefully, all would be revealed on Monday when we would begin our intensive library research. I was quite excited at the thought.

Mark picked up the extortionate bill. The cost was somewhat irrelevant; it had been the most perfect evening, and everyone had thoroughly enjoyed themselves.

Slightly tipsy and uncomfortably full, we left the friendly embrace and charm of the hotel to return home. The silence of the echoing, cobblestone street was broken by five unruly adults staggering noisily side by side.

Fumbling aimlessly, Mark finally managed to insert the obtrusively big, iron outer door key in its lock; the door opened. Five minutes later he miraculously succeeded in finding the second elusive keyhole. Opening the door with a discourteous slam, we all piled in.

"Are there children living next door?" Eve innocently enquired as the routine patter of miniscule feet conducted their opening performance.

"No, it's empty next door," I replied quickly, staring questioningly at Mark. "Shall we have a little nightcap before bed?" I said cheeringly, likening myself to Freida next door who had also rapidly tried to change the uncomfortable subject.

Mark proceeded to pour five full shot glasses of strong liqueur, each of us chinking quickly before swallowing the warming liquid. We chatted for a while longer, enjoying another flowing glass. Fred happily joined us, revelling in all his newly acquired attention. Even Mark remarkably picked him up for a cuddle. I definitely put this down to him having had one too many during the course of the enjoyable evening, and even put a stop to him trying to take him upstairs to our bed.

With little Fred safely tucked up in the solitude of his cozy nest, we retired for the night. I tucked the giggling girls up in their cold double bed. Not mattering their older years, I still did it; their smiling, happy, albeit tipsy faces peering back at me from the crisp white bed linen. They loved it too; I was sure. The icy chill of the room slightly subdued with the help of the electric heater.

I affectionately blew a kiss at George from his bedroom doorway. Yawning heavily, he was still fiercely interacting with his mobile.

I walked quietly up to our bedroom. Strangely, I wondered how Alice was going to feel tonight now that the cottage was in its full occupancy.

CHAPTER TWELVE

I felt my body being nudged suddenly. I pulled the duvet hard over my half-naked shoulders, a knee-jerk reaction to my constant battle every night with a husband who self-indulgently feels the need to wrap himself up like a sausage roll. Another ill-mannered prod followed. Instantly, I sat up, petrified that I had a ghost violently trying to cause a confrontation.

Blearily, I opened my eyes. A mug of hot steaming tea came into my sight along with Jen.

"Good morning. Wow, thank you; what a lovely surprise!" I yawned, carefully placing the hot mug onto my bedside table. "Did you sleep all right?"

"Mum, it's six in the morning!" She laughed.

"Six?" came my exhausted reply.

"This is one noisy house: banging, creaking floorboards! How do you guys get any sleep round here?" She moaned albeit in a cheery fashion.

"You get that in old cottages. The old timbers almost groan at you," Mark, now awake from his slumber, expertly replied.

"You're not kidding there; spooky shit!" she said, flouncing hastily off to the bathroom.

I looked at Mark's sleepy face, stroking his cheek. We lay back down, our pillows greeting what seemed like their old long-lost friends. We cuddled, oblivious to everything around, enjoying the warmth, peace and tranquillity that our bed had to offer.

We both decided to get up, relishing momentarily in each other's safe havens. The enjoyable moment, however, was seized from us by the rising of all three, apparently exhausted, children; none of them having slept particularly well, due to the constant boisterous bumps and bangs that the cottage projected at us.

Fred bounded up excitedly, playfully wagging his miniscule, curled up stump of a tail, totally engulfed in his happiness to see everyone. We drank hot mugs of tea and coffee as we watched the early morning news. Walking down the stairs beforehand, I had noticed our newly repaired wedding picture. It had been moved; it was now face down on the mantlepiece. I annoyingly made a point of positioning it back to its rightful place.

Leaving the others downstairs, I went up to wash and dress, tidying each of the rooms along the way. I neatly laid out the girls' clothes, that had been strewn on the floor the night before, on the bed, placing them tenderly down.

Unexpectedly, I caught a fleeting, eerie shadow in the doorway. Fearlessly, I gazed straight towards it. Slowly and surely, the apparition began manifesting into that of a pale, transient image. A small child eventually stared solemnly back at me, golden hair in tight ringlets. I stared in disbelief as the little girl we had seen in the grainy photographs had suddenly and unbelievably come to life.

Gasping, I stepped back. I wasn't at all frightened, just extremely bewildered. The child timidly backed away. I followed patiently, with each gentle footstep edging their way gingerly towards her tiny frame. I slowly lifted my hand, gradually reaching it out towards her, trying desperately to gain her trust. It didn't work; she turned and swiftly ran up the corridor. Quickly, I pursued not really knowing what to expect next. The ghostly spirit, now a fluttering shadow, diverted into the smallest bedroom.

Before reaching the doorway, I stopped dead in my tracks. A weird sound distantly echoed from the room, a jingle jangle toneless tune, clattering in an obtuse, clumsy way. As I took a fearful step towards the entrance, the noise got unnervingly louder. Apprehensively, I peered into the sinister room; there was nothing other than the continued piercing noise which seemed to be originating from under the bed. Petrified and standing like a zombie, I really did not want to look there. In every horror movie I had ever seen, something scary always managed to appear beneath a bed.

With all my inner strength, I hastily flipped the covers away from the side of the single bed where George had slept the night before. The alien noise deafeningly continued. Terrified, I stooped slowly down until my frightened eyes met with the terrifying depths of darkness. In the deepest, murkiest corner, which it just had to be, I saw the outline of a thing; this strange entity was banging cymbal-type objects obnoxiously together in an unharmonious atrocious manner.

As my fearful eyes hastily adjusted to the dark lighting, I jerked backwards in realisation and comprehension of what I had just seen. It was one of those grotesquely hideous monkey toys dressed in an unattractive yellow, green and red waistcoat with a matching frightful hat, clumsily banging away on its cymbals. I immediately felt nauseous; frightful toys appearing out of nowhere and switching themselves on was not in the least bit acceptable.

I ran to the bathroom next door, where the mop was conveniently standing. Grabbing it violently, I thrust the end at the horrid, monstrous contraption, prodding it brutally and with all the aggression I could muster. A faint whimper of a cymbal clash finally escaped its grisly being, followed by a whirring, to which I gave another almighty poke. I swear I heard it cry. Exhausted mentally, I went and sat on our bed.

Mark came in a couple of minutes later to dress. "Are you okay?" he asked concerned, obviously noticing my shocked and clearly visibly upset appearance.

"No," I whimpered pathetically. "Look under the bed in George's room!" I gestured to him to go and look.

Mark turned and walked up the hall in a calmed silence. The mop still lay in its abandoned state, half in the bedroom and half out in the hallway. He picked it up and leaned it against the bedroom wall. I stood nervously, waiting in anticipation immediately behind him. Bending down onto his knees, he slowly peered under the bed looking aimlessly in all directions.

"Over on this side!" I directed, pointing towards the left of the bed, the pillow end.

"I can't see anything, Ann. What am I looking for?"

"What do you mean you can't see anything?" I barked frustratedly, switching the light on to help. "Look in the corner!"

"Ann, there is nothing there; come and look yourself." He huffed crossly, knees creaking loudly in objection as he struggled to get up from the obviously uncomfortable crouched position.

I bent down hesitantly and stared to where minutes earlier I had brutally slain the offending atrocious creature. Nausea once again fluttered through my empty stomach as I squinted at the now empty void under the bed. My husband was right; there was absolutely nothing there.

"Mark, there was this ghastly little toy monkey playing its hideous cymbals. I had seen Alice, and I followed her into this room, and that thing was under the bed making its revolting noise!" My voice falteringly mumbled. "I shoved the mop into it until it shut up," I continued, my eyes almost pleading to be acknowledged.

"Where is it now then?" Mark said, as he looked around the room exasperated.

"I don't know, Mark," I replied, feeling my eyes welling up with frustration.

"Come on, it's okay; I believe you. Let's forget about it for now, enjoy the day with the children, and tomorrow we will investigate this further." He gently put his arm around me as he spoke, kindly reassuring me at the same time.

I felt moderately better as he cuddled me, dejectedly wiping my salty, dismal tears away. I placed the mop back into the bathroom and splashed my flushed face with tepid water. Was I actually going mad, I thought as I gently patted myself dry with the soft hand towel. I had definitely seen and heard that revolting nasty little monkey, but why hadn't anybody else? It had certainly been loud enough. I cross-examined myself over and over until crestfallen I went back downstairs.

Fred followed me into the kitchen, and almost immediately, my dismal thoughts were lost as our adorable little puppy bounced in and around my feet. Preparing yet another feast of a breakfast, I busied myself, burying the earlier disturbing events in the darkest chambers of my mind.

Happily, I laid the table, and we sat eating vast amounts of unnecessary food, until all of us felt that uncomfortable, pointless feeling of fullness. We cleared the table and dishes as the children went upstairs to change from their pyjamas into their clothes. I prepared everything that was needed for our roast dinner later, peeling the assortment of fresh vegetables and parboiling the potatoes. Generously stuffing the huge chicken, seasoned with plentiful flavours, I wrapped it loosely in foil before placing it gently in the warmed oven.

The sun was shining brightly. It was a stunningly beautiful autumn morning, the glowing reds giving a magnificent display of colours in the immense number of trees.

We decided that we would take a pleasant stroll round to Gallows Bridge and embark upon the picturesque walk, which would take us around the perimeter of the castle. Fred, I had been informed, had already received his final set of inoculations, so we decided we would take him on his first walk in his new little village. It was a long walk, and I doubted that he would even manage half of it, with his tiny legs incorporating his podgy fat frame.

Half an hour later we were all finally ready to go. We locked up the cottage and the noisy gaggle made its way up the country road. It was Mark this time who paused to look up, and with the kids walking on ahead of us, he stopped me to look at what he could see. The wistful, pitiful face at the top of the window peered back at us, doleful, vacant eyes, staring bleakly in our direction. The image was much clearer this time, the same as when Alice had appeared to me in the morning.

"Elisabeth!" we both said spookily in unison, turning briefly to look at each other in disbelief.

Our eyes returned magnetically to the window. Unsurprisingly, the face had disappeared, the curtains once more gaping to one side. I heard Mark draw a sharp intake of air and exhale almost aggressively as we continued walking, not wanting to alert the children who had carried on, obliviously giggling their way ahead. We didn't speak; we didn't have to.

"We may have to consider getting a priest or someone round to carry out a sort of exorcism," Mark whispered subduedly, interrupting the dark silence.

"I think that we need to find out the actual reason the cottage is being haunted, first. There has to be a good explanation as to why the ghosts haven't passed over to the other side," I replied seriously. "Before approaching a priest, we need all the information that we can lay our hands on; otherwise they could think we are incredibly stupid!" I continued as Mark nodded enthusiastically in agreement.

"Yes, and you know how gossip spreads around this village!" he said, laughing scornfully, raising his eyebrows sharply upwards.

We continued to walk, rejoining the children up ahead. Fred bounded along happily, causing me to almost trip over his untrained, dog walking manner. We passed the pretty cottages and their everchanging abundance of appealing flowers, each basket or pot overloaded with a variety of plants and rainbows of colour. Stopping for a few moments, we took time to appreciate the radiant sight.

Further ahead, we arrived at the scenic bridge. Fred paused nervously at the shallow river edge, it's gentle trickle of water steadily and delicately flowing along. He wasn't quite sure what to make of it. Eventually deciding that it would be good to drink, he clumsily sunk his squashed little face deeply in. The deceiving coldness of the water took him completely by surprise, together with his nostrils being filled to the brim. He shook himself intensely whilst sneezing at the same time, and he tumbled over backwards narrowly avoiding a total dunk in the cold invigorating water. We all laughed as he embarrassedly regained his composure.

I took several photos and asked a friendly passerby if he would kindly take one of us as a family group. He took a few to be on the safe side. Thanking him, we continued with our long walk towards the castle.

The trickle of the river breezed aside us as we drifted blissfully along. It was pleasantly warm in the autumn sunshine. We followed the narrow, bramble-lined path until reaching the lovers' bridge, and for a short time, we stopped to admire the breathtaking views. I sat with Fred on the small, snug seat meant for couples in love. Appreciating the temporary breather, he began snoring the moment his weary body sat down.

I carried my tired, lightweight pup as we continued to make our way towards the scenic colourful landscape of the castle grounds. We had taken the children into the castle on a previous visit prior to our permanent move. They had marvelled at the elegance and magnificence that the public rooms on display within had to offer. The grounds themselves were dramatic and never ceased to delight me, each visit as captivating as the last. It made an appealing walk, albeit a moderately tiring one for the not so fit or able.

On reaching the other side, we arrived back in the quaint, historic high street, where we all agreed a quick glass or cup of something would be more than acceptable. The hotel welcomed dogs, and seeing as Fred was totally exhausted from his long maiden journey, I could see him being no problem or annoyance to any of the other guests.

We sat in a considerably cramped fashion around the welcoming flames of the fire, the children managing to obtain vacant stools from around the bustling bar. Sunday lunchtimes were always popular in the hotel; they served a first-rate roast dinner, although a touch on the expensive side. I could never warrant spending that sort of money on something that could be made so cost effectively at home.

"Well, it's been so nice to see you all," I said as we chinked our mixture of glasses and coffee cups in agreement.

Finishing, we made our way back home, the smell of the roast chicken cooking, reaching our hungry nostrils as we opened the door. Immediately, I put on the rest of the dinner, conscious of the fact that the children had a long drive back home.

We sat eating with everyone surprisingly hungry again after having had such a huge breakfast earlier. The children engaged happily, enjoying each other's company, together with the home-cooked food. Most of all, it had been superb to have them spend the quality time with us.

All too soon, it was time for our family to depart. They gathered together their belongings and gave Fred huge forever cuddles. Closing the door gently behind us, we walked them to the car, hugging and kissing tenderly each of them. We were sorry to see them go; it never seemed to get any easier, saying our goodbyes.

Eve backed her Mini carefully and slowly from the drive with Mark guiding her onto the road, windows down. We waved them off until we could see their flapping hands no longer. Knowingly, Mark pulled me to him, his strong arm enveloping my waist. We both shed silent, private tears as we walked back into our home.

CHAPTER THIRTEEN

Setting the alarm extra-early to prepare for the onslaught of the workforce, morning arrived all too soon. I wondered whether we should leave Fred with all the disruption that would be going on in the cottage, but swiftly decided it would be unfair to put him through the trauma of the constant commotion. He would have to come with us.

Seventy thirty arrived together with a constant stream of men. Mugs of tea in hand, Mick explained to us the schedule of intended works that would, hopefully, be completed during the course of the day. Everyone admired the inquisitive little bundle of ugliness that was sat comfortably in my arms.

Mark and I gathered all that we would require for the day of banishment from our own home. This mainly encompassed items for Fred. We decided that we would take him for a long walk by the sea once we arrived in town, in the hope he would then sleep, his needs not indifferent to that of a baby.

At just gone eight thirty, we loaded ourselves together with Fred into the car and took an extremely slow drive towards the coast. The sky was full of dark, murky clouds. I hoped fervently that the rain that they clearly threatened to bring, stayed within. It didn't look overly promising to say the least.

We paid for a day's parking at the desolate pay and display car park. Over excited and full of beans, Fred managed, somehow, to tangle himself hopelessly up in his lead. I left him on the seat trying to escape his self-made confinement, giving us time to organise our bags and outerwear for our long day ahead.

We had earlier placed the photographs that contained any information in a brown envelope. Comfortingly, I patted my bag, confirming that they were still there.

Bracing ourselves for what was going to be a chilly walk ahead, we left the car and made our way along the perimeter of the golf course, the sand dunes forming part of the foreboding landscape. The gusts were strong, as we were facing full exposure of the elements. Poor Fred was having an increasingly hard time with it, losing his balance frequently in the ever-strengthening gales.

The waves were crashing fiercely down on the beach, the stones clashing noisily as the ebb retired, waiting impatiently to roll into the next fearsome surf. Pulling my woolly hat around my protected ears, my hair still managed cleverly to whip into my eyes, stinging as the salt-ridden strands whipped furiously back and forth.

Making our way down towards the beach itself, the sand dunes gave the luxury of some shelter against the battling winds, taking the brunt of the gusts that swirled around us. We were protected in the shadows of the tall sandy mounds, the walk now, so much more pleasurable. Fred, however, wasn't quite sure about the sand. Having overcome the problem of the gale force winds and the terrors of the swirling, angry seas, he was now confronted with this strange itchy stuff which he decided would be tremendous to eat. A squashed face, plastered in grainy yellow shingles, he looked an absolute picture and a dirty, grubby one at that. He was less than impressed at the oppressive grit in his mouth and nose, sneezing on and off relentlessly for about half an hour after.

We turned back after quite a long stretch, feeling exhausted as the wind continued to play combat with us. At the end of the golf course, thankfully, there was a tap at which, to Fred's utter disgust, I managed to wash him down, leaving us once more with a freshly laundered, if not a bit bedraggled pup. We had a small towel in the car, and I rubbed his shivering body dry, before wrapping him warmly in his little checked woven rug. He appreciated all the snugness that the cosy blanket had to offer, and after a few snacks, he instantaneously fell asleep.

We took the opportunity to have a hot drink and made our way to the little café. The kind owner allowed us to bring our sleeping pup in, as he was unnoticeable and encased in the snug shopping basket that I had bought entirely for this purpose.

We embraced the warmth of our coffees. Feeling slightly peckish, Mark ordered us bacon rolls, and a quick refill followed, before making our way to the library. I hoped that they would allow Fred in and debated naughtily whether to just hide him in the basket.

The library itself was situated at the far side of the town, and a good fifteen-minute walk. It was now eleven thirty and relatively peaceful everywhere. We arrived at the mammoth information centre, and hoping for a sympathetic receptionist, I decided to be honest. I respectfully asked whether it was possible to bring our sleepy puppy in. The bespectacled young girl took an admiring glance at the cute Fred sleeping blissfully in his shopping basket and nodded her seal of approval as long as that would be where he would stay. I thanked her, assuring her wholeheartedly that it would be.

We found a small table, conveniently tucked away with computer access. Placing Fred unaware underneath, we made a start on our investigations. Mark wandered off round the vast number of aisles containing countless rows of books. He located a few large editions, detailing the history of the village going back through the ages. He flicked through, every now and again pointing out something that, whilst fascinating enough, had absolutely no relevance to our search.

With the bespectacled girl's help, we located the microfilms from the *Western Gazette* dating for 1890 to 1910. She helped me load them into the viewer. It was a laborious task, sifting through the infinity of pages filled with an abundance of irrelevant information. The newspaper covered an extensive area. On the rare occasions our village was mentioned, it was, more often than not, an event at the medieval castle or a wedding. This was going to take a lot longer than I initially thought.

Mark's computer ability was particularly questionable, but he too painstakingly searched for any information that would lead us to solving the mystery of our haunted cottage. It was proving fruitless for both of our hard endeavours. My neck was aching with stress; I kept leaning back and circling my head in a clockwise then anti-clockwise direction, trying desperately to loosen the ever-increasing knots of anxiety angrily building up from within. I had reached the year of 1900, when suddenly a small article caught my tired eyes:

The wedding of William John Wraith and
Elisabeth Mary Hyem took place today,
at The Priory Church of St George

The date was the 14th of October 1900. I quickly printed off the page, pleased with my very significant, minor step of progress. I left the viewer to show Mark my diminutive finding.

"I have found this; nothing much!" I said, handing him the print. "It's really slow going," I continued, peering in at the still-sleeping Fred.

"It's a start and more than I have found," he replied despondently.

I left him and carried on looking at the monotonous and repetitive articles, column by column, page by page. It was mind-numbing work. Three long hours had passed with only the marriage detail to show for it. Our time was constrained as Fred wouldn't be asleep for too much longer. I was disillusioned and disheartened, thinking begrudgingly that it should have been so much more straightforward.

Mark came over with the rustling shopping basket, an inquisitive head peeking out from the top of it. "I think it's time for us to go," he said, nodding down in the direction of the now very excitable Fred. "I will take him outside, while you pack our stuff up."

"Okay, I won't be long," I said, as I hurriedly gathered all our bits and pieces together.

I left the area tidy and located our bespectacled friend, thanking her appreciatively for her patience and help. I also intimated that we may return in the morning, thus, gaining authorised Fred entry passes.

Outside, Mark was being led a merry dance by the mischievous Fred. I rescued him hastily, before an accident pursued, deciding jointly to take our bundle of energy for another longish walk. It was four o'clock, and whilst strolling along, we debated whether to return home.

"Let me call Mick for an update, and then we can decide from there," Mark wisely suggested as he took his mobile from his jacket pocket.

He called. Mick answered almost immediately, giving a full and detailed description of all the work that had been completed during the course of the day. Having encountered a few more problems than had initially been anticipated, which were expertly overcome, there still remained a fair bit to accomplish. The builders were currently finishing bits for now. Tonight, however, he informed Mark we would be without heating and hot water. My husband expressed his thanks, saying we would see him in the morning. He came off the phone and relayed the conversation to me which I'd pretty much got the gist of.

We arrived back at the car, and Fred ate his dinner from his bowl on the concrete. It didn't seem to bother him in the slightest, as he noisily pushed it around in circles, snorting and grunting like a pig in the process. There was a cheap and cheerful pub in the town centre which happily accepted dogs, so after demolishing his food, we walked our full, barrel-bellied pup in the opposite direction that we had walked in the morning, towards the line of beach huts. He bounded frantically along, doing his business on the way, his podgy little frame, once again, bearing the full brunt of the still-existent gales.

"I'm actually starving!" Mark said as we walked past the huts and onwards towards the Jurassic cliff tops.

"Me too, and I'm knackered!"

We laughed as Fred crisscrossed between our legs.

"Let's wear him out, and then we can enjoy our meal in peace," Mark said as we made the most of the rapidly diminishing light.

We walked for as long as we possibly could with the daylight swiftly fading. It was becoming increasingly unsafe to walk the cliffs for any longer, so we turned back, Fred once more suitably walked.

Just before arriving at the pub, I scooped the tired pooch into my arms, wrapping him tightly in the comforting folds of his blanket. Placing him down gently in his comfy shopping basket, we entered the pub, finding a lovely little table for two.

Mark returned with our drinks. It had been an exhausting day and not yet confirmed, one that would probably be repeated tomorrow.

"I wonder if the builders came across our ghosts today?" I said, laughing scornfully, sipping my chilled glass of wine.

"It had crossed my mind earlier, I have to say!" Mark said, laughing loudly. "I expected a phone call at any minute saying they had left the building!"

We giggled, as we tried to make light of our weird situation.

Reality hastily kicking in, I spoke. "I was really terrified yesterday morning, when that despicable thing started bashing its bloody cymbals under the bed, then the next minute it disappeared! That spooked the shit out of me," I almost whispered, my laughter rapidly subsiding.

"I know you were, and I do believe you. We have both seen stuff. The important thing is we need to stick together on this and resolve it as soon as possible!" Mark paused. "Maybe they don't like the change."

"Hmm, I think you're right. That could explain why the cottage's previous inhabitants lasted only six months! It probably wasn't marital problems at all!" I answered.

"I think we may as well come back tomorrow. Let's both go through the newspaper pages. It will be a damn sight quicker and, hopefully, might prove more productive!" Mark proposed, even though I already knew that I would be returning anyway.

Hungrily, we ordered our meals from the surprisingly cheap menu. It was busy for a Monday and clearly a good choice with the locals, which ultimately was always a good sign.

CHAPTER FOURTEEN

The day began much the same as the previous one, with the builders overtaking the cottage at an alarming rate. Mick spent over an hour guiding us through the completed works, together with the outstanding stages yet to be accomplished.

New gleaming radiators were now in place, together with the newly fitted modernistic boiler; all would apparently be up and running during the course of the day. The kitchen, however, would take a few more days. It was an empty shell at the moment with the base units being fitted today. The bathroom would be the last for completion as certain pipework had to be rearranged to accommodate the more modern-style fittings.

Gerry the silent decorator had carried on in the areas he could without disturbing the other more constructive work. Today he would begin painting the tired exterior as the weather forecast appeared to be good for the next few days. The low morning sun was already streaming through the windows.

We gathered up everything we needed, and with an excited Fred afoot, we set off for a repeat performance of the previous day. Arriving at the same desolate car park again, it was like déjà vu; out bounced Fred yapping excitedly.

Today there was no wind, and although marginally fresh, the glorious bright sunshine shone down, making it almost feel like summer. We walked for ages admiring the stunning coastline. The waves gently lapped onto the shore; a vast difference to that of the previous few days when they were totally uncontrollable, ravaging beasts.

We walked the eager Fred down to the edge of the sea. He'd overcome his irritation of the sand, flicking it happily in the air. The water, however, fascinated him, stepping cautiously in, then immediately bouncing out as the calm waves gently licked the shore. The random larger waves, appearing out of nowhere, would frequently catch him out, soaking his naive little body in the process.

Walking happily in the sunshine, I appreciated again why we had moved. On Sunday, I'd had reservations, with all the ghostly disturbances; and more so, when we had said our goodbyes to the children, I had yearned to go home that night, aching to be closer to my family and our previous normal life.

The upsetting incident with the monkey tipped the scales. I had felt like giving up and walking away from it all. After all, who in their right mind would want to live in a house full of ghouls?

That morning, I had looked up the meaning of poltergeist on the internet. It was derived from two German terms: *Poltern*, meaning 'to knock' and *Geist*, meaning 'spirit'. I just wanted to be rid of all the paranormal activities. If nothing could be achieved from our research, then I would call in a priest so they could exorcise once and for all the multi-dimensional beings that crazily persisted in manifesting in our home.

We arrived at the tap and quickly washed Fred's salty and sandy fur. He was more agreeable to the procedure today as the sun was warming his body at the same time. Walking back to the car, we laughed as Fred stumbled behind us, dragging his bottom on the floor, clearly wanting to give up and walk no further. Managing to almost drag his weary little frame to the car, I scooped him up and wrapped him in his comfy little haven. Immediately, he buried his head, instantaneously falling asleep, exhausted once again from his long morning stroll.

Arriving at our favourite little café, we greeted the owner, who was an adorable little Italian man in his fifties. He ushered us to our seats and took our orders. Taking off our coats, we sat down, contemplating our work ahead. We decided that continuing the trawl through the vast amount of newspaper articles would be the best course of action, agreeing that anything vaguely of significance would surely reveal itself there.

Our coffees and toast arrived, and hurriedly, we finished them, keen to get stuck into our difficult search that lay ahead. Thanking the owner, whilst paying our bill, we left and made our way towards the far end of town to where the library awaited us.

The bespectacled girl, thankfully, was once again on reception. I pointed to Fred asleep in his basket, out of politeness, to which she mouthed, "No problem." Once again, she set up the newspaper microfilms with each of us able to view separate screens.

Taking our seats and Fred safely tucked out of sight, we began our monotonous task: silently and painstakingly, we studied each of the numerous pages intently.

I found myself straining over each page, desperately trying to find anything that would help us piece this complicated puzzle together. I wanted to resolve it, no longer having the patience left to continue being gracious and fed up with having to turn a blind eye to our awful situation; furthermore, resenting the fact I was having to sit in the library for hours trying to gain snippets of information. No matter what sad story the phantoms had to tell, I wanted them out of our home.

It wasn't long after, that the second piece of the jigsaw popped up for Mark's attention.

Mr & Mrs William Wraith are pleased to announce the birth of their first child, a daughter named Alice Florence Wraith, on 2nd January 1901.

Excitedly, Mark pointed at the article, once more printing it off for our pile of meagre evidence.

"So, Alice is their daughter then?" I said, staring at the editorial with interest.

Putting it down onto the desk, we were encouraged, and our searching continued a little more enthusiastically.

An hour passed when Mark discovered the next item:

Mr & Mrs William Wraith are pleased to announce the birth of their second child, a boy named William Junior Wraith, born 4th April 1903.

"Okay, so there was a baby brother too. Come to think of it, there were a couple of pictures with a baby in," I said, as I desperately tried to recollect the images in the extensive number of photographs that we had previously gone through. Putting the paper alongside the other and pleased with our progress so far, we carried on once more exhilarated and refuelled by our finds.

Mark stretched his neck upwards, groaning loudly. He wanted to take a break. A couple of hours had passed with no further articles coming to light, and the constant straining over the screens was extremely taxing.

"I'll go and get us some takeaway coffee," he said, bending down to tenderly kiss my forehead.

"That's a good idea," I agreed gratefully.

Fred was still content under the desk, enjoying his deep, peaceful sleep. It was quiet in the library with not another soul in sight. We were able to concentrate, undisturbed and with no distractions. It was actually a really nice environment to be in, and I decided that I would definitely continue to make use of its seemingly unlimited facilities and information.

Suddenly, a large article on the front cover of an edition in 1907 caught my eye as well a picture of a little girl, Alice! The headlines stated:

Dated 16th June 1907
GIRL FOUND MURDERED
The body of six-year-old Alice Florence Wraith was found murdered yesterday afternoon in the bedroom of her home. The mysterious circumstances

surrounding her death have left her family devastated. Police are currently investigating a sighting of a young man seen running from the scene shortly after. Her father, William Joseph Wraith discovered her body. The cause of death is still said to be unknown.

I sat back, completely shell-shocked, Alice's haunting face staring vacantly back at me. I felt sick, as I reread the piece over and over. I turned to the next page which was dated the 17th of June 1907. The following article read:

HUNT FOR CHILD'S KILLER CONTINUES
Police are still investigating the murder of young Alice Florence Wraith and are today continuing their search for the young man seen running from the scene of crime, described by the girl's father, William Wraith, as tall, dark haired, wearing tweed knee-length breeches and matching jacket, around sixteen years in age. Villagers are advised not to approach this young man as he is deemed extremely dangerous. Police will be releasing a statement within the next couple of days confirming the actual cause of Alice Wraith's untimely death. Police are also asking for any witnesses to step forward with any further information.

I was struggling to take the information in as I rapidly scoured the next edition for more information.

Dated 18th June 1907
CHILD RAPED AND SUFFOCATED
Police have now confirmed that Alice Florence Wraith was sexually assaulted and suffocated with a pillow. The six-year-old was subjected to a horrifying ordeal. Police are once again appealing for any further information, on a confidential basis. They will be continuing their intensive search with door-to-door questioning.

There it was, the horrendous, sickening truth. I was numb inside, not really knowing what to think.

Mark returned, happily holding steaming hot coffees. His mood immediately sorrowed as I pointed the articles out to him. "Oh, my goodness!" he mumbled, as he read through the awful pieces. "That's terrible, absolutely awful." He sighed heavily, trying to absorb the information in front of him.

I scanned through the following pages, printing off any information that was relevant. Articles appeared on the days following Alice's murder, including, seemingly pointless interviews from neighbours and shopkeepers. Given the information in the editorials, we gathered that the mysterious sixteen-year-old had only been seen by William Wraith, with no other witnesses or any further information coming to light.

Mark's mobile vibrated on the desk. It was Mick the builder updating him on the day's progress. The boiler and heating were up and running. The kitchen units were mostly in and would be finished off in the morning. Mark came off the phone and once again relayed the conversation I had just heard.

"I have had enough today,' I said, putting our printouts in a pile.

"Same," Mark replied, as he packed up his stuff. "It's been hard going, hasn't it?" he said, slipping his arm around my shoulder, a show of appreciation and acknowledgement of the horrible information that we had successfully uncovered.

We left the library feeling very subdued. I awoke Fred, who affectionately licked my hand as I gently stroked his soft little head. Almost immediately, he was out of his basket ready to take on the world. We decided to repeat yesterday's excursions, and with the weather being so fantastic, we agreed to make the most of it.

As soon as we stepped outside into the brilliant sunshine, I felt lifted, the warmth of the sun rays feeling wonderful on my face. Feeding Fred again in the car park, we set off once more for the incredibly stunning cliff tops. The views as we walked were breathtaking, the astounding jagged cliffs, jutting defiantly into the deep turquoise waters of the sea. The waves were breaking onto the cascades of rocks at the base, with floods of white foam floating freely in the air.

The sheer drops below were spectacular and not for the fainthearted; the coastal path in places had dangerously eroded away. The weather, together with harsh storms over many years, had taken their toll. The superior cliffs had an almighty presence, and walking along them usually gave the ultimate, therapeutic experience. Today, however, we walked on in deathly silence; our thoughts were occupied with the sad fate of poor little Alice Wraith.

With Fred appropriately worn out once again, we took a slow meander towards the cheap pub we had visited yesterday. With the builders probably still in situ and the kitchen in a semi-unusable state, it seemed the obvious option to take. We sat at the same table as the previous night, like the creatures of habit we are. Fred was reluctant to crawl into his basket, so he sat happily, taking in the surrounding environment; every now and then, enjoying the clumsy affections of the customers, drunkenly asking what breed he was.

We sat with our drinks, and eventually Fred tired of all the attention, bored of the constant hard patting of the head and the aggressive rubbing of his chin. Climbing into his shopping basket, he hid himself away from all the unwelcome advances.

We put off ordering from the huge menu, as my appetite had unsurprisingly disappeared. We discussed the day's findings, still horrified at our sickening discoveries. My mind was in complete overdrive.

"That's why the top bedroom is constantly cold and the door is always open," I said, breaking the heavy silence. It was Alice's bedroom; that's where she was murdered." I paused briefly, before continuing. "Her baby brother would have had the small room where George slept," I surmised thoughtfully.

"I would agree with that," Mark answered, gulping back his pint of black stuff.

"How awful must it have been for the family, Mark?" I questioned, shaking my head disbelievingly. "Maybe Alice is trying to tell us that she was murdered?"

"But then that's nothing new to what people would have already known," Mark responded rationally. "There must be more to it?" He rubbed his head thoughtfully before disappearing for a much-needed cigarette.

I thought of the image of her mother in the back dress, more than probably taken at her daughter's funeral. I continued to contemplate as I sipped my wine. The manifestation of Alice that both Mark and I had encountered was that of her around the age of six, the age she had actually died. It suddenly dawned on me: Elisabeth's haunted face at the window and in the photographs; she looked barely more than a child herself.

We ordered another drink before finally deciding to order some food. Our conversation filled with the mysterious Wraiths and their unfortunate events. We continued on, as we ate our meals, finally appreciating our lack of food that day.

"Looks like we will be back tomorrow?" Mark laughed, as he scraped his fork around his empty plate.

"Well, I had thought that I would be coming back. I wasn't really sure that you would have wanted to do the same thing yet again?" I looked at Mark questioningly.

"Ann, we will be coming. We need to put the rest of the jigsaw in place," he spoke firmly.

CHAPTER FIFTEEN

Once again, the morning arrived with the hustle and bustle of the brash builders. I was actually grateful that we would be disappearing out of the house for the entire day. The cottage itself was looking stunning; the exterior had been painted a brilliant white, such a difference from the grey and faded drab colour that it was. The transformation was amazing; it looked like a different cottage entirely.

The heating worked perfectly, and the radiators were now so quiet compared to the bangs and groans of their previous counterparts. The kitchen was shaping up nicely too with most of the carpentry work completed. Slowly but surely, the cottage was being deeply cleansed, it was becoming our own.

The ghostly occurrences had settled down slightly over the past couple of days. The door at the top, I now left open; it seemed a pointless exercise closing it every night, when in the morning it would just be upsettingly, agape again. My handbag was continually moved from the sofa under the stairs. There was, undeniably, something bizarre about that particular area of the room. It was almost guaranteed that whilst in that zone, I would virtually, unfailingly catch the briefest glimpse of an evanescent shadow disappearing up the stairwell.

After chatting with Mick, who so far had done an exceptional job, we collected our things for yet another day of coastal walking and painstaking searching in the library. Fred waited patiently at the door; he knew he had a fun day ahead.

The sun was glorious once more. It was an even better day than the previous with not a trace of any wind, the warmth of the sun rays falling onto us as we strolled along the calm edge of the sea. The gentle waves lapping tenderly onto the shore, the beach was desolate, and the peacefulness was tranquil. We enjoyed the solitude that it offered us, both deep in thought, not really wanting to speak.

Fred was in his element, playing the game of tag he had invented yesterday with the uncompromising waves. We walked further, finding it extremely exhilarating. The isolated beach gave us the space and escapism that was so desperately desired by our increasingly fragile states of mind. We held hands as we turned back, strolling slowly along the frothy water's edge, embracing everything that the beautifully bright autumn day had to offer us.

Fred knew the routine and sat patiently, shivering under the tap waiting for the cold fountain of water to rid him of the intrusive substance coating his matted puppy fur. He shook himself, drops of icy water spraying and covering everything around him. I wrapped him in his blanket once we reached our car which was parked in its now regular spot. We headed for the café, where we ordered coffee and toast, the same as yesterday.

Hurriedly, we finished, eager to resume our tiring research. I didn't really know what we were going to gain from our knowledge or, more importantly, what we were going to do with it. Today we needed to discover little Alice's mysterious killer.

The bespectacled girl greeted us like long-lost friends as we entered her domain. Like yesterday, the library was also deserted, and I think she was probably appreciative of the presence of two beings, albeit entirely miserable ones. She set us up without even asking, leaving us in our solitary confinement.

There our slow process began, once more, meticulously scaling the pages and reading every single article in case we missed the slightest little thing. The endless pages of news gave me a thorough insight of our area in the 1900s, but it was mundane in comparison of what we really needed to find out.

From the initial discovery of Alice's murder, the articles appeared daily, getting smaller and less detailed as each week passed. The police were still investigating, but with no further witnesses and no further information regarding the young boy seen running from the scene of crime, they had nothing to go on, as the days turned into weeks then months. The case, sadly, remained unsolved.

As I moved onto the next page, the following article raised my shackles. I nudged Mark sharply, and we both read the passage in silence:

Dated 29th October 1908

Dated 29th October 1908
**MOTHER OF MURDERED CHILD ALICE
WRAITH COMMITS SUICIDE**
**The body of Elisabeth Mary Wraith was discovered
hanging in her home yesterday afternoon by her
long-suffering husband William Joeseph Wraith
who only last year discovered the body of his
murdered daughter Alice; the case today still
remains unsolved. Mrs Wraith left no note, and
police have confirmed they will not be investigating
the circumstances of her death any further.**

We both sat utterly dumbfounded and in shock. It was
a while before I could speak. "How terrible, and poor
William, losing his wife and daughter." I sighed heavily.

"It's hard to comprehend the amount of pain and
suffering he must have gone through, isn't it?" Mark
responded quietly.

"She must have been totally distraught over Alice's
death to have taken her own life and to leave her little son
without his mother," I said, as I continued to trawl through
the following pages.

"Her grief must have been unbearable," Mark
responded, craning his neck over my screen. "To kill
herself, she was obviously inconsolable."

"Why are they haunting our home though?" I
questioned, looking at Mark's frowning face.

"I don't know, Ann," he replied. "Maybe at the time
Elisabeth committed suicide, Alice's murder had still been

unsolved. Let's keep looking; we need to find out about Alice's murder."

We continued to search through the articles, examining the pages carefully. As the years passed by, Alice's murder remained unsolved, the articles becoming few and far between until filtering out completely. Police had left the case open. Their enquiries had led to a fruitless end, with the mysterious disappearance of the sixteen-year-old, dressed in tweeds, seen running form the scene of crime.

"I think we may as well give up, don't you?" I said to Mark, as my neck once more ached with stress.

"Yes, I don't think there is anything more to be gained from this now," he agreed, stretching his back out from the knotted position. "Let's go."

Packing up our things, we thanked the bespectacled girl, who seemed genuinely upset that her only customers were leaving somewhat prematurely. We trundled outside, with the bemused Fred ready and alert for another piece of action. The cliffs were the obvious choice, so we grabbed a takeaway coffee on route before embarking on the tough climb upwards, where the outstanding scenic coastline would greet us.

Fred sauntered along happily as we chatted about our findings, the grassy cliffs exposed to the strong bright sunshine. Unusually, there was no breeze. Being at such heights, the wind was almost guaranteed, but not today; it was absent, leaving me sweating in my outerwear designed to protect against the elements.

We decided that today we would take Fred to the hotel as the cheap pub had exhausted its options to us, the novelty of the cut-price menu rapidly wearing off. The hotel was not exactly economical, but the luxurious surroundings, together with the cosy atmosphere far outweighed the sad, basic environment that the cheap pub had to offer. Returning to the car park, we fed a ravenous Fred, then drove home to drop off the car.

Mick greeted us in the driveway as he loaded up his van with heavy bags of tools. We invited him to join us for a drink at the hotel, so that he could update us on the day's events. As we were chatting, I caught Freida's inquisitive face staring out of her window; I waved at her. Suddenly, it occurred to me that she must have known about the Wraiths and their sad fates. I made the decision that I would pay her another visit, sooner rather than later.

The builders had finished for the day. Subsequently, we decided to leave the exhausted Fred at home; he was more than happy as he snuggled his tired little body up, revelling in the home comforts that his own bed had to offer. We locked the two doors and walked up the cobbled high street, glancing up as always to our window; there was no face present today.

We found a spacious table for three. Almost immediately, Mick joined us. He gave us a fully comprehensive report on all the progress so far. The work was on schedule as he had initially planned, with no further unforeseen problems occurring. The bulk of the renovations would be completed by the end of the week.

This news pleased us, not wanting to feel like spare parts in our own home for any period longer than necessary.

"Have you noticed anything strange in the cottage?" I blurted out unexpectedly, as Mark almost choked into his drink.

"What do you mean strange?" Mick responded. His bushy eyebrows rose slightly.

"We think its haunted," I said straight out, looking at him directly in the eyes.

"Haunted?" He paused for a moment or so, slowly sipping his beer. "Come to think of it, I had noticed a few random bangs upstairs, when there was none of my boys working in that area." He placed his glass back on the table. "That would be the only thing I could say that was odd."

"We have noticed that too. You have lived in the area a while; had you heard anything about the history of the cottage?" I said, continuing my gentle probing.

"No, can't say I have," he replied, shaking his head. "Why do you ask?"

"We found out that a child was murdered in the cottage and that her mother had committed 'suicide not long after," I said calmly, as the two men gulped back their drinks in shock.

"Bloody hell!" came Mick's traumatised reply. He stammered, "That's terrible."

We continued to talk about the strange happenings that had been occurring. It had felt good to offload our experiences on the poor, now-involved builder, but he listened in fascination as we explained our appalling list of discoveries. It was almost a relief that we could actually talk to someone about it, without sounding eccentric or even weird.

Mick proved to be an extremely good listener, his caring demeanour continually present throughout. He mentioned that he had an elderly aunt who hadn't moved from the village in all her long life, and he would go and visit her and see if her memories could recollect anything that may give us answers. Our newfound friend also had a vast number of contacts and would make discreet enquiries on our behalf.

The hour-long conversation gave Mark and me revitalised confidence. We had felt earlier that we'd reached a dead end, an unmoving formidable barrier. Now we had renewed hope, and with Mick now on board, we were stronger, more mentally able to cope with this abnormal thing that we'd had the misfortune of moving in with.

We bade Mick a fond farewell, thanking him gratefully for his moral support and the help that he was kindly offering. A subtle code of silence held firmly in place, he walked away, leaving us alone to gather our thoughts.

"I think we did the right thing there," Mark said. "It was nice to tell someone, without them thinking we are mad."

"He might be able to help us," I replied, hopefully.

I felt so much better, a huge weight lifted from my heavily laden shoulders. I knew that my husband felt the same, his sombre mood so much more uplifted. The recent events had taken their toll on us both, at a time when we should have been revelling in our newfound happiness, not spending umpteen hours researching in the local library looking up morbid events, especially ones that had the audacity to have taken place in our own home. I wasn't even sure any more that I wanted to live in a place that had been subjected to such horrific incidents.

I questioned my ability to actually continue on. Even if we were to rid ourselves of the resident manifestations, would we be able to remain there with our knowledge of those dire happenings? Would we ever be free of the overwhelming gloom and dark shadows that our cottage had looming over it? However much we changed, renovated or cleansed our new home, the sad fact remained: it hid an abysmal past.

CHAPTER SIXTEEN

Sitting in our sweet-shop window, we stared despondently out. Once again it was a glorious day, the sunshine already peeking cheekily through the branches of the trees. The builders had already begun their morning ambush, the noisy cluttering and banter going on around us. The obligatory radio was on, blaring out obnoxiously in the barren kitchen.

Fred ran around like a headless chicken. He sat by the front door at first waiting for his coastal walk, eventually realising that this was not going to happen today. He ran around everyone, his tail wagging furiously as he was shown obscene amounts of attention. Little trails of wee followed him. It was a good job it was on their dust sheets, I thought smugly, watching the little wet patches appear.

Calming down eventually, he plonked his chubby little backside down on my feet underneath the table. I decided that this morning I would pay Freida and Albert a visit. They had to know something, having lived in the village all their lives. They were in their eighties after all. This would have meant they were born in the late twenties, early thirties. Surely, village gossip would have reared its ugly head at some point during their lifetimes.

I told Mark of my plans. He was in total agreement, telling me to take all the paperwork and photographs as evidence. A few odd jobs needed to be done, which he'd been detracted from doing as the library trips had taken priority. Pottering around and avoiding the areas of mass destruction, he began his little list of chores.

I cautiously put in date order all the newspaper articles which we had printed. Carefully going through the piles of images, I picked out all the relevant ones that would aid me in my conquest to obtain further valuable knowledge. I wasn't entirely sure how I would broach the subject with the cagey pair; it would need a lot of discretional tact and a patient understanding of the elder generation.

Gathering up all my weapons, I left the house and made my way up the path of our neighbour's cottage. Taking a deep intake of breath, I knocked sharply on the door, feeling nervously anxious at the same time.

Albert greeted me with a warm smile. The waft of bacon reached my nostrils as he led me into their busy little kitchen. Freida immediately sat me down, and before I knew it, a steaming cup of strong tea was placed in front of me together with a plate of her homemade shortbread.

Placing my folder in a business-like way onto the table, I breathed in sharply. "Freida, Albert, I have something very important to ask you."

I paused, inhaling deeply, my shoulders rising up in anticipation. "I have information here..." I patted the folder in front of me before continuing, "Evidence, that a child was murdered in our cottage during the early part of the 1900s, and then shortly after that, her young mother committed suicide."

I stared intently at Freida as I spoke, watching for the faintest reaction. Her face stared back with no emotion. "Did you know of these events?"

I watched Albert glance uncomfortably at Freida, his face flushing a furious pink. He nervously looked at the floor, fidgeting uneasily with his buttons.

Freida patted her apron down, taking a few seconds to speak. "We did," she replied, not offering any further information.

"What do you know?" I questioned abruptly, thinking that it was going to be exceptionally difficult to obtain anything from this strangely evasive woman. "Albert?" I looked towards the clearly flustered elderly man.

"Err," he began to half-heartedly stutter, his edgy, oversensitive manner clearly visible to all.

"We know the same as you," Freida interrupted tersely.

"Did they find the murderer?" I persevered, rapidly losing my dwindling patience.

"No, they never did," she replied, uninterestedly.

I paused, trying to retain the anger that was rapidly building up inside of me. She was being particularly cagey and blatantly concealing something. My frustrations were increasing at an alarming rate. I felt the anxieties of the past days rising within my body like a volcano about to erupt. Freida, I felt, was being deliberately obstructive with me, and there was absolutely no way I was going to leave until they gave me what I'd gone there for. I positioned myself for a new battle.

"Do you know what became of the father and son?" I glared at the uncooperative woman in the eye.

At this point, she squirmed visibly, her frail body almost reeling back in a twisted contortion. I watched as Albert reddened even further, his agitated hands obviously clammy. Opening my folder, I confidently placed the arrogant picture of William Wraith immediately in front of Freida, watching her intently as she recoiled, dumbfounded in her seat; her face distorting as she tried to regain her rapidly disappearing composure.

"William Wraith passed away in 1935," she said, her usually direct voice quivering slightly. "I can tell you the exact date; it was the 29th of December 1935." Looking down at her lap, she continued with barely a whisper, "It was not long after my eleventh birthday."

I was now very confused. Freida had gone from being painstakingly evasive and obstructive to slowly become a fountain of knowledge, providing precise dates. How did she know so much? I questioned myself, waiting silently for her to speak again.

"You're wondering how on earth I can remember?" She looked at me knowingly.

I stared blankly back at her, astounded that she'd somehow just read my mind. "I was actually," I replied quietly, nodding for her to continue.

"William was my father." She spoke in a flat emotionless voice.

To say I was totally gobsmacked would have been the understatement of the year. This new information was flooding through my brain, a terrifying rollercoaster ride, taking me to the highest peaks, then bringing me back to the lowest of lows. Albert shuffled around uncomfortably as we sat in a sombre, subdued and awkward silence. He poured us another tea, which I was tremendously grateful for as my dehydrated mouth was parched dry.

"How did he die, I hope you don't mind me asking?" I managed to splutter out, keen to hear more.

"He had a problem with his heart." She spoke sadly, clearly upset with the memory. "Our mother struggled to cope after he passed, and so my eldest brother John became the man of the house – he was eighteen at the time – working all hours that God would send, so that he could provide food for our table." She paused, as she recollected her sad past. "My youngest brother, Charles, was fifteen when my father died, and he took it very badly, going inward and sulky. He barely spoke to a soul after.

"What happened to your father's first son?" I questioned, absorbing every piece of information like a sponge.

"Well, he was twelve when my father married my mother; she took him on like he was her own. The following year, John was born. William Junior became jealous and aggressive towards the new baby. Not long after that, he was carted off to his Aunt Marie, where he was to stay. We never saw him after that.

"Oh," I said, my mind doing somersaults as it slowly tried to decipher this deluge of intriguing information.

"Did your father ever talk about Elisabeth and Alice?" I bravely questioned, feeling that it was indeed a delicate subject.

"Never!" she almost snapped. "Their names were not mentioned in our household. We found out, only by listening behind closed doors." She smiled wryly at the memory.

"They never found the murderer then?" I said, shaking my head.

"No, pet, they never did." Freida stood up, immediately. I took that as a sign to leave. She looked pale and exhausted.

An overwhelming wave of pity swept over me for her. "Thank you so much, Freida; it must have been very difficult for you, and I'm sorry for putting you through this again." I gave the frail old lady a hug in appreciation as I softly spoke, her body flinching tensely as I did so. She clearly was a very cold, detached person.

Strolling down their pathway, folder in hand, I felt that something had at last been achieved. The mysterious murderer still remained unidentified, but a whole new jigsaw had begun to take shape. I was desperate to see Mark and give him my news.

CHAPTER SEVENTEEN

I walked into the monotonous sound of drilling and banging, the radio still blaring crudely, loudly, probably to itself. I found myself huffing rather loudly towards the unintentional intrusion. I located Mark who was precisely adjusting our stubborn wardrobe doors, which seemed to have a mind of their own, shutting only when forced, a bit like the obnoxious, top bedroom door.

"Hello, you," I said, kissing my husband's hot, furrowed brow.

"Hiya, how did you get on with our delightful neighbours?" he asked, a fraction sarcastically.

"I have actually got loads of information, after an evasive struggle," I whispered smugly, like a cat that got the cream. "Do you fancy a coffee at the Water Mill? I will tell you all about it."

"Yes, definitely, let's go. We can take Fred with us; he's been a total nuisance, getting under everybody's feet all the time." Mark stood up, his knees creaking loudly as he did so.

I caught the faintest shadow on my right-hand side, then nothing; it disappeared almost instantly. Ignoring the brief manifestation, I called Fred. He came bounding out of nowhere and sat surprisingly still as I put on his lead, his little tail enthusiastically wagging, nineteen to the dozen.

Walking down the lane, we passed the quaint, picturesque cottages on our right. A little old lady was bent down tending to her pretty gardens. She looked up as we passed by, politely acknowledging our presence.

We reached the Water Mill. It was an impressive building built in 1680 and remarkably still in working order, another small tourist attraction that the village had to offer. I sat on one of the benches in the tranquil gardens, basking in sunshine, the river Avil flowing gently by. It was always such a peaceful setting and totally unspoilt this time of year, with barely a soul around.

Mark joined me, arms laden with a tray of coffee and freshly made egg mayonnaise sandwiches. We tucked in, with Fred completely fascinated by two mallard ducks climbing playfully in and out of the water, the husband-and-wife tag team managing to attract his attention fully as I began relaying Freida's captivating story.

Mark sat in total awe as I quietly spoke, telling the tale exactly and with absolutely no details left out. He didn't say a word as he listened intently, astounded at the new twist in our unravelling mystery. I finished speaking and waited patiently for my astounded husband's response.

"Bloody hell!" he finally spoke, his head shaking disbelievingly from side to side. "I wasn't expecting you to say that."

"It's incredible, isn't it?" I replied, taking a large bite from my untouched sandwich. "I really don't think we are going to find out the identity of the elusive murderer though, not if Freida can't even tell us."

"But why are they haunting us then?" Mark said, greedily shovelling in the last mouthful of his sandwich.

"There has got to be an explanation," I replied thoughtfully.

Mark finished off the rest of my sandwich as my appetite had curbed somewhat. Although the sun was out, it was becoming slightly chilly in the shade. We left the peaceful setting of the garden and followed the path towards the lane. Fred scampered happily along, enjoying his little piece of freedom.

My mind was brimming with the newfound information that had been learned from our secretive neighbours. I wondered why Albert had acted so uncomfortably, until swiftly coming to the conclusion that they must still be concealing something. I had to capture Albert, a task which would be exceedingly difficult to fulfil as he barely left the clutches of his wife's taut apron strings. If only I could grab an opportunity to pose a question to him, he may well find it arduous to evade. This could be our only hope. I decided satisfactorily that this would be my next mission.

We arrived back home; the noise, unfortunately, hadn't subsided. I sat in my perfect sweet-shop window, swiftly allowing myself to become wrapped in my own oblivious little cocoon. Resuming my research, I typed the word 'ghost' into the search engine on my laptop. Various pages quickly appeared. I opened the first that looked to be the more informative one.

'How to spot a ghost' popped up intrusively. *Not that difficult in this house,* I thought sarcastically to myself as I began to silently read through the paragraphs. 'Shadow people, human-shaped mist, transparent human forms.' *Yes, we have definitely experienced more than our fair share of that phenomenon,* I thought before continuing. 'Feelings of being watched.' *Yes,* I nodded enthusiastically at the laptop in agreement, probably looking like a complete idiot to anyone that happened to be watching me.

According to the various pages of endlessly repetitive information, it seemed that we were unquestionably experiencing every sign of a haunting possible. It seemed to be quite rare, however, to come to close contact with the full-blown manifestations which Mark had encountered in our bedroom doorway and me in the top bedroom. We had only seen the face of Elisabeth at the window, unless she was the fleeting shadow that kept appearing in the corner of my eye, disappearing instantaneously, the moment I would turn my head in its direction.

I then read with interest, numerous supposedly real-life stories of alleged sightings, some unbelievably unthinkable in their nature; tales of demons possessing the bodies of their innocent victims. In a strange way, I felt somewhat privileged that our ghosts were seemingly friendly, albeit weird.

It appeared that Ghostbusters or Paranormal Investigators, as they preferred to be known, would carry out pretty much the same significant research as we had already completed. They would thoroughly investigate the allegedly haunted site, making in-depth enquiries about the sightings, including times of day, signs of repetitive behaviour patterns and any prominently obvious hotspots. One thing that we hadn't actually even contemplated was fitting up cameras around the house, resulting in capturing any images or poltergeist activities that may or may not occur.

Significantly, it then crossed my mind that if we were to call on such people for help in this matter, then we would have to supply them with some form of evidence to authenticate our encounters, other than our staid collection of newspaper articles and dull sepia photographs, which was all, in fact, we currently had in possession. Somehow, we would have to create a trap, possibly recording or photographing the unusual occurrences that were happening constantly around us.

My mind instantly began to ignite with ideas, desperately trying to map out a clever strategy. The handbag on the sofa was probably the first place to initiate a start, I thought quickly. Delighted with my own self investigating, hurriedly, I jotted down some notes, planning my clever course of action. This evening, I would set up my camera in the faintest hope that I could capture an image which would clearly demonstrate the proof of evidence we needed.

I hastily resumed my research on the laptop. A boldly accentuated word caught my eye: 'Séance'. I clicked onto it. 'A meeting at which a spiritualist attempts to receive communications from the spirits of the dead.' I shuddered visibly reading the words and rapidly dismissed the page out of sight; it gave me the creeps even thinking about it.

That was not going to happen in our house at any stage and however desperate we were.

I continued clicking the limitless links which looked even vaguely interesting, feeling totally motivated and driven towards my obtainable goal of dispensing our new home of these unwelcome malevolent 'shadow people'.

Fred unexpectedly interrupted my train of concentrated thoughts as he began barking erratically at nothing in particular on the stairs, his upright ears pinned back apprehensively and his hackles bristling. I clicked on 'Strange animal behaviour', scanning the page at speed. I read: 'Dogs may obstinately refuse to enter a room or cower in a pensive manner without any apparent reason.' Fred definitely hadn't got to that stage yet, I thought to myself triumphantly, almost like it was a competition that I was clearly winning.

Feeling very lethargic, I walked into the noisy kitchen where I managed to locate the kettle. Wiping the layer of dust which had managed to find its way onto every possible available surface, I rinsed it out. Having a quick body count of males in the vicinity, I began to pour cups of tea, handing them out to the seemingly neglected and now grateful workforce.

Sitting back down in my haven of solitude once more, I stared vacantly out onto the road, picturing Elisabeth's dark face probably also staring out of the top window. Sipping my hot tea, I meticulously began to type out a full journal of everything that had happened so far: all dates, approximate times and a detailed description of any occurrences, however minor they may seem, since we moved into the infested cottage.

Taking several efforts, I managed to summon Mark down from his chores upstairs, asking him to read scrupulously through the comprehensively detailed chain of events. Straight away he found a few discrepancies on the list to which he carefully amended, and surprisingly, he added a couple of extra 'shadow people' sightings that I had no prior knowledge of.

We argued, as I was quick to question the fact that he hadn't previously informed me, then I backed hurriedly down with the stark realisation that I'd kept most of my 'little' incidents from him. Lowering our voices to a mere whisper, we discussed the vast list in the sombre realisation that we weren't alone.

CHAPTER EIGHTEEN

As my clearly drained, both physically and mentally, husband closed the door on the last of the bumbling, dusty builders, I began the daily laborious task of wiping down and cleaning all the surfaces of the dirty particles that had consistently layered them during the course of the day.

Lighting some overpoweringly strong, cinnamon-scented candles to take away the persistent paint and wood fumes, I started to prepare our evening meal unusually with no music to interrupt my silent little world. The sounds of the children playing next door eerily didn't bother me; I just added it into my ever-increasing journal of occurrences. Strangely enough, Mark failed to hear them.

We sat down to a healthy meal of fish, new potatoes and fresh leeks, both of us ravenous having eaten only the polite egg mayonnaise 'afternoon tea' type sandwich quarters earlier. I discussed my researched plan of action with my bemused husband as we ate, debating and arguing on the most desirable position for the now fully prepared and ready-for-action camera.

Clearing away our spotless plates, we set a mini tripod up on the now clear table, directly aimed so the image would cleverly capture the notorious handbag spot on the sofa, the floor where it ended up in the morning and part of the creaky stairwell, the definite home to the notorious shadow people. It was insanely awkward trying to peer into the lens like supple contortionists aiming for their most ultimate position. Eventually, we finally agreed on the seemingly appropriate spot, and we both smiled in a self-righteous way as my high-tech camera was cleverly positioned in its place of rest. It had the capacity of recording, if set on a timer which was triggered to capture even the slightest of movements. I wondered to myself why we hadn't done this before.

We sat watching the TV in subdued silence, somehow managing to enjoy the serenity our freshly decorated home now had to offer. The builders' full-on invasion every day although extremely worthwhile was horrendous, with absolutely no privacy or peace available in any shape or form to take comfort in. We still had a few more days of intensive labour to go, and that was being slightly optimistic; then, however, our dream home would once again be in our possession, other than the creepy, foreboding apparitions that continued to assault the place.

Once again, I heard the faint noises of the children innocently playing. I looked over at Mark who was nodding gently, sleep clearly taking its toxic hold. Physically drained from the odd jobs he had accomplished throughout the day, he was completely oblivious to the muffled sounds. Who were the children? I questioned myself uncomfortably as I stared upwards in the direction of where the noises were coming from. I wondered why it was only me that mostly encountered them.

Gently, I nudged Mark's now snoring body and together we switched everything off, carefully locking all the doors. My handbag, the main character of the plot, was set on its centre stage with the timer set to capture any alerts or movements.

Pulling the covers around me and wrapping my arms around my husband's broad torso, I felt safe and snuggly, enjoying the warmth that both our bed and bodies had to offer, subtly ignoring the unwelcome sounds that the groaning cottage was constantly making. I made a mental note to add them into my journal.

I woke abruptly and stared vaguely at the florescent clock face on my bedside cabinet, gradually coming into focus; it was two thirty in the morning. Immediately, I wondered if our filming had been a success, wanting desperately to have a quick look, almost like an innocent child at Christmas urgently needing to see their present-laden sack. I ignored the yearning as the darkness scared me at night. There was no way on earth that I felt an urge to bump into any spook or chance meeting a 'shadow person', however young and harmless they may appear to be. It definitely did not appeal to my better nature. The safeness of my covers enveloped my body, shrouding it in a guarded off-the-limits fortress.

The morning eventually came; my sleep had been disturbed relentlessly since my initial wakening at two thirty. I felt utterly exhausted as I dragged myself up, pleased, however, that it was finally morning and that I didn't have to continually wrestle any more with my overpowering, unsleeping mind. My thoughts and ideas seemed to go into overdrive at night, misbehaving in the knowledge that it should be their time to slumber.

I quickly dressed in preparation for the arrival of the army of builders and their battalion of noise. Pleased to see me, Fred wagged his tail happily on the bottom step, the noise of our movements upstairs clearly awakening his tired little body.

As I made my way down the creaky staircase, my glance was immediately drawn to the camera set so firmly in position on its previously sturdy tripod. I stared hard; the camera lay on its side with the strategically placed stand now in pieces. There was absolutely no way it could have fallen; it had blatantly been tampered with. I grabbed my mobile phone and took a couple of pictures of the aftermath, to add to my growing pile of evidence, mad at myself for having not taken any of it being initially set in place.

A sharp knock on the door disturbed me as I reviewed my shots. Once more the obnoxious attack began as the hardworking, beleaguering team began their painstaking work for the day. Gerry the silent decorator, lost in his own world of oblivion was the only one that seemed to enjoy quiet, losing himself in the few semi-tranquil positions in the cottage, peacefully left to his own devices.

Forgetting initially about my handbag, I turned to look at where it was usually located every morning. Surprisingly, the bag was still perched on its centre stage waiting for the performance to begin. Very strange that for once it hadn't been moved; our little ghostly fiends were playing games with us.

Mark came down the stairs. Discreetly, I showed him that our clever little plan had failed, with me whispering and pointing fingers at the discarded camera and mini tripod, then towards the failed handbag stunt. Fortunately, the camera itself was still intact, so I began to fast forward through frames to see if anything had actually been captured. An hour into the grainy footage, a blurred commotion began to appear fuzzily on the screen, followed then by murky, still darkness. Unbelievingly, it was almost as if it had just fallen over.

My mind started to barrage me with endless options. We would have to set it up again that night. The camera would need to be wedged so it was rigid and totally unmovable. I looked around the room, my eyes darting about in the search of items to use as a sturdy vice. A couple of heavy books would probably do the trick. If the camera was placed firmly in the middle with the books strategically placed either side, there would be absolutely no way the camera could fall or move unless pushed. I tried it, using Mark's massive golf manual and my huge recipe book, both of them being the heaviest I could lay my hands on. I created a deep cavern, putting the camera firmly into position. I shook the table hard; nothing moved. Again and again, I repeated the action; nothing was shifting. My experiment had been successful.

Pleased with my innovative idea, I made cups of tea for the now gasping builders. Mick was taking Mark on his daily morning tour of work in progress. He hadn't mentioned our 'haunting' conversation since our night in the hotel, but I noticed him looking at me strangely as I

148

carried out my weird camera trial when he'd passed through the room.

I decided to continue on with my mundane research. Mark still had ample jobs that he was going to get stuck into. It also made common sense to do so whilst all the continued disruption was going on. My seat in the sweet-shop window was a perfect little haven amongst the organised chaos clattering around me.

Sitting in my favourite spot, Fred came to join me, placing his podgy little bottom expertly on my comfortably soft slippers, clearly bored and exhausted from the all the tireless attention received from the workforce.

Mark disappeared upstairs to embark on his hard day's work. I began to update my journal, logging full details of the dismal failed bag trap, so carefully set up the night before. It wasn't entirely relevant as nothing sinister had happened. There was no ritual moving of my handbag, which had been the whole point of the façade, and certainly no appearances of the 'shadow people' fleeting this way and that.

I typed in the word 'ghost' again. There were countless pages and articles to go through, and yesterday I had barely even touched the outer perimeters. It seemed continually repetitive with the various sites almost copying each other's information. There were countless referrals to the famous poltergeist films, reportedly based upon real events. Other true-life stories made enthralling reading, including fairies, elves, vampires and werewolves. They all seemed, on the most part, exceptionally far-fetched and were beginning to raise the hairs on the back of my neck as I stupidly continued to read the bizarre revelations.

One paranormal site showed pictures of supposedly ghostly images, a number of 'orbs' captured in shots were blamed on high camera exposures and were mostly deemed as fake. Numerous shots of haunting dark shadows pictured under trees with no valid explanations or reasons available, seemed to be continually repetitive.

Dark faces appearing in mirrors seemed to be another popular image with various justifications attached to each of the pictured shots. Reflections and bad lighting were thought to be the probable cause of these ghostly images.

The fake picture of 'Nessie' the Loch Ness Monster suddenly sprang to mind as the image had caused years and years of controversy. The constant conspiracy theories and, still to this day, the ongoing film documentaries covering a simply elaborate and very clever hoax.

I went back to the task in hand, swiftly moving on from my totally unrelated distraction. I clicked on the word 'Demons' and started to read through the limitless grisly articles, boundless tales of bordering on horrendous human possession and ghastly exorcism. I shivered outwardly as the supposed actual events became harsh reality in my graphic and already disturbed mind. Surely these beasts and monsters going back to the dark ages couldn't physically take over a mortal's body? I found it difficult to believe some of the nonsense appearing before me.

Standing up, I slowly stretched from my uncomfortable, hunched position, deciding it was tea-break time for the troops. I felt the urgent desire for space to gather my increasingly distressed thoughts. It was difficult for me to comprehend and decipher all the shocking revelations; and to actually think that some of the stories were apparently reality and based upon real-life experiences was unbelievable to me. I felt extremely spooked and desperately vulnerable as I set to work making the huge round of teas.

Mark came down from his haven upstairs and helped me hand out the steaming hot mugs and plates laden with biscuits. "How are you getting on?" he enquired, eventually joining me in my refuge of sanctum.

"I'm scaring myself stupid, reading all these ghost stories and hauntings," I said with a pained expression.

"Don't read them any more, not if you are getting yourself worked up and petrified in the process," Mark suggested sensibly, as he dunked his tenth biscuit in his tea.

"Are you hungry by any chance?" I asked, laughing, as he displayed signs of obvious gluttony. "Make some toast or something more substantial."

"No, this is fine, just what was needed. I want to crack on, have too much to do today." With that, he disappeared, mug in hand, upstairs.

I ignored his levelheaded advice, dunked another biscuit and clicked on the word 'Exorcism'. This unsurprisingly began to highlight countless links. I began to read:

'In January 1999, the Vatican issued a revised Exorcism rite to be used by Catholic priests. The directions for conducting an Exorcism comprise of a single section in the *Roman Ritual* (one of the books describing the official rites of The Catholic Church).'

I paused briefly, studying the article with significant interest.

'To perform the rite, the exorcist dresses in his surplice and purple stole. The ritual of exorcism is then, mostly a series of prayers, statements and appeals.'

I continued reading:

'In addition to these recitations, the priest takes certain actions at specific times during the rite. He sprinkles holy water on all present in the room, lays his hand down on the subject, makes the sign of the cross both on himself and the subject with a Catholic relic. The Lord's Prayer is also recited.'

It was pretty much as I had thought and now something that I was absolutely determined to have done in our precious cottage.

I stared vacantly out of the window, completely lost in my own little transparent world. Freida and Albert walked by and politely waved. I ignored them unintentionally as my daydreams held court as I failed to notice their obvious presence. I finally managed to wave in realisation, when they had already walked by.

My thoughts hastily resumed to our situation. I had conjured another plan of action. Tonight the camera would be set up again, and the evidence would then be optimistically captured. Then in the morning we (I would tell Mark this later) would take a walk down to the village church and ask the Vicar, or whomever was responsible, for advice on our strange and totally absurd situation. I hoped that our words would be taken seriously and the help that we needed would become available to us. Surely the church would be our saviour. Somehow, I realistically thought it would not be that easy.

Evening arrived surprisingly quickly, the last of the builders expertly loading up their vans, leaving us once more within our domain of solitude. Fred went outside and played happily by himself in the courtyard as we began the cleaning routine once more, giving the quick 'once over' to everything in sight. Dinner tonight was to be pasta with tuna and sweetcorn, a simple dish to make in our almost-finished kitchen.

Once again, we polished off our food, starving at having only eaten biscuits all day. After dinner we decided to walk Fred up the high street for some much-needed fresh air. As Mark rubbed his nose, his funny front door locking habit, I heard the children. We crossed the road, and hesitantly I turned to look up; the darkest glimmer of a shadow disappeared from the newly parted curtain. It happened so quickly, I wondered whether or not I had actually imagined it.

As we walked slowly along the cobblestones with Fred bounding happily along, I pondered on why that window in particular was a regular sighting for Elisabeth's dark, almost-transparent face. It bothered me that it was our bedroom. Why did she keep appearing there? Who killed Alice? The questions raced uncontrollably around in my head. I felt weary and exhausted trying to fathom out the mysteries our new home was unravelling. This was a special time that we should have been happily revelling in our wonderful new cottage. I felt resentful and angry that it was being spent in frustrated terror and absolute uncertainty.

We reached the top of the hill and decided spontaneously to have a quick drink at the hotel. It was a much-needed tonic as for once we actually spoke about anything and everything other than our ghosts. Mark was in good spirits, thoroughly pleased with the amount of work he had accomplished during the course of the day. Deciding to stay for a second drink and changing the subject back to our morbidly dismal apparitions, I explained my need and determination to seek the advice and possible help of the church as soon as possible.

"I thought about walking down to the church in the morning, Mark. Will you come with me? I don't want to sound like an eccentric mad woman in front of the priest." I asked, blatantly to the point. I sat patiently, waiting for my husband's delayed and thoughtful reaction.

"Yes, of course; we will both sound like eccentric idiots then," he said, to my utter and upmost relief.

"Hopefully, we can capture some form of evidence on the camera tonight to take with us," I responded optimistically.

"That bloody bag is moving on its own every single night. At some point we will surely be able to capture something on film." Mark paused aggressively, taking in a large gulp of his Guinness. "Something or somebody is doing something, and we will get to the bottom of it. It's really beginning to get to me now, and I've had enough."

I was ecstatically pleased with my husband's sudden positive and determined outburst, his strong mindedness powerfully dominating the conversation. Finally, he was undeniably taking it on, and together we would face our demons.

CHAPTER NINETEEN

The next morning finally arrived and I almost ran downstairs. The night before we had both carefully set up the camera in its pole position. There was absolutely no way that it was going to move. The camera was meticulously wedged between the heavyweight books. We also added a hefty encyclopaedia behind for good measure. A triangle-shaped cavern locked our weapon firmly in place. I took photos of our work to add as evidence of what we were trying to achieve.

As I reached the middle of the staircase and stared towards the pile of unmoved books, my gaze was drawn to my bag. Surprisingly, like the previous morning, it remained untouched. My stare returned swiftly to the table. The camera was missing; the cavern was void.

"Mark!" I screamed uncontrollably, before slowly walking down the remining steps. Mark came running with lightning speed as soon as he heard my anxious wail.

"The camera is gone; it's missing!" I looked at my husband's confused face as he tried to take in the clarity of the situation.

We both examined the empty cavern that we had been so blatantly proud of the previous night. I quickly glanced around the room and under the table, my eyes desperately scouring the highs and lows. The camera was nowhere to be seen. Running hastily to the kitchen and the back lounge, I scanned the furniture, shelves and floor. Mark was doing the same. We ran upstairs and began to examine each room, briefly running our eyes over every possible area that the camera could now be.

As I entered our still-dark bedroom, I pulled back the heavy curtains to let in the light. I stared down at the freshly painted windowsill, and there it was, the camera in the exact same spot that the manifestation of Elisabeth regularly appeared to be stood.

"Mark!" I called my husband.

Entering the bedroom quickly, he walked over to me, and we stared in shocked silence at the offending camera. It bothered me immensely that the poltergeist had not only managed to remove the camera, it had floated it upstairs and entered our bedroom, our safe domain. I began shaking, and tears began to roll down my flushed cheeks, as the unsettling reality began to set in.

Mark put his arms around me, consoling my completely traumatised state. He angrily took hold of the camera, huffing loudly as he did so. Pressing the button, we checked through the frames, watching patiently as nothing whatsoever appeared. He pressed the rewind button and studied it intensely again, in the faintest glimmer of hope we might have missed something.

"Nothing," he said in totally irritated disgust. "We will have to try it again tonight; this thing is not going to beat us."

I agreed, still violently shivering with shock. Quickly, I dressed as the builders would be arriving at any minute.

Feeling emotionally drained and altogether very scared, I felt as though our beautiful dream was falling apart in thousands of pieces scattered around me.

On hearing the knock at the door, Mark went downstairs and welcomed the now dwindling workforce, giving me much needed time to emotionally pull myself together. I heard Mick arrive and their muffled voices droning through the walls. They both took me by surprise as they abundantly entered the bedroom.

"Ann, Mick has some news for us," Mark said, his ashen face seriously solemn. I glanced quickly at Mick. He was following behind Mark initially and had now moved forward to speak. I gulped loudly, apprehensive of what he was going to say.

"Morning," he said in a subdued way and not in his normal brash manner, continuing on, "I went to visit my elderly aunt last night, the one I told you about, at the hotel. I asked her about the Wraiths." He paused momentarily.

"What did she say?" I almost whispered, urgently.

"She said that apparently rumour had it that William Wraith was eventually accused of the murder of young Alice, but there was never enough evidence to convict him of the crime." He stopped briefly, before adding, "He was the only one that saw the so-called murderer running away from the cottage; his word against no one else's."

Exactly at the moment Mick mentioned William Wraith, I saw a 'shadow person' appear to my left, at Elisabeth's window. I quickly turned around towards it, but the whispery mist had disintegrated into thin air.

"Unfortunately, there is a bit more to it, Ann," Mark added, with a stern tone in his voice.

"Gossips in the village apparently started to surmise that William Wraith had actually killed his wife too, as the way she was found hanging would have been impossible for someone of her slight build to have accomplished. There would without doubt had to have been a third party involved." Mick exhaled heavily, waiting for my dumbfounded reaction.

"What do you mean, the way she was found hanging?" I gasped, barely managing to speak.

"She was found hanging from the stairwell, a stool was kicked away from her feet. She would not have had the strength or been able physically to have hoisted herself into that position; her body was barely the size of a child."

I listened in total horror as Mick relayed the harrowing information which would have meant that it was William Wraith that had raped his own daughter and taken the life of his own innocent young wife, cleverly, making it look like suicide, in the knowledge she couldn't cope with the gruesome mortality of her daughter. I felt sickened to the pits of my stomach with our new addition of unwelcome knowledge.

Unsurprisingly, I heard the children as the story was being told. Had we disturbed them, bringing back the terrors that had occurred in their one-time village sweet shop? I brushed the annoying ghosts from my mind.

"Why wasn't he charged with the murders?" I questioned disbelievingly, my mind in petrifying limbo.

"They had no evidence whatsoever. He was apparently an extremely noble person in the village, and it was brushed under the carpet, so to speak," Mick replied, shrugging his shoulders haphazardly.

Mark who had remained strangely silent throughout, gratefully shook Mick's hand and thanked him for the very important missing jigsaw piece. Mick left us alone to try to comprehend the terrible scenes that had almost certainly taken place in our lovely new home.

"I can't stay here any more, Mark," I spoke, my body shuddering continually. "I mean it."

"Let's not rush into things. I do understand how you feel; let's go somewhere private to discuss what we now know." Mark gently took hold of my hand as we gathered up Fred and our coats. I really couldn't get out of there quick enough. The visit to the church would have to wait.

We drove slowly through the high street in subdued silence. Upon reaching the main road, I burst into tears of frustration and shock. Mark continued to hold my hand as our poor, bewildered puppy looked confusedly on.

We arrived at the seafront and decided to take the exhilarating cliff walk to clear our minds of the cobwebs that were now festering angrily away. Fred didn't care where he went as he tugged happily on his lead, pleased with another opportunity of experiencing freedom once more. We began the long steep walk up the cliffs. The bitter wind was strong again, whipping around our exposed faces. The odd tears escaped and rolled down my cold cheeks. Mark noticed and affectionately brushed them away. We stopped, and he hugged me firmly, his large frame overpowering mine; and for that short space of time, I felt momentarily safe.

"Right, let's think about what we now know," he said confidently, releasing his body from mine. "We need to go over each room and finely piece together all the paranormal activities that have occurred in those particular areas." He turned to look at me, awaiting my seal of approval.

"Okay," I replied forlornly, secretly wanting to totally give up on everything.

We decided to finish our walk first, then discuss and make notes over lunch at the cheap pub. Home was the last place I wanted to go, so was extremely grateful of any suggestions that would keep me away longer. The blustery wind was making the walk acutely difficult; it was problematic enough trying to negotiate the ragged, unruly cliff edges, especially with a pulling, inquisitive puppy on our hands. The coastal path could be particularly unforgiving in places, and we needed our wits about us as we were being blown threateningly along.

A couple of gruelling hours and an exhausted puppy later, we arrived back at the car. Fred quickly gulped down his water as if he had been walking in an arid desert and had just discovered an oasis. He then polished off a handful of dry food. I pulled out the shopping basket, which he associated immediately with bed. Climbing in happily, his gruff little snores started almost immediately as I wrapped his cosy little blanket snugly around him.

We walked to the cheap pub, stopping on the way at a stationery shop to buy a notepad and a pen, which absentmindedly we had neglected to bring in our somewhat hasty rush to leave the house. Continuing our walk along, we found the town surprisingly quiet for the end of the week. The weather blowing a fierce gale probably didn't help, I thought to myself as we entered the usually bustling pub. We found a private booth in a corner which would enable us to have a quality, uninterrupted conversation and, more importantly, understand what we now needed to do to move forward or alternatively back. I wasn't entirely sure that I wanted to continue living at the cottage. It was supposed to be our wonderful dream, a fresh new start for both of us. The harsh brutal reality was, it had become a continuing and worsening nightmare, which we couldn't awake from.

We ordered cappuccinos so that we could warm up our chilled bodies. Pulling out the notebook and pen, we began our assignment of deciphering all the evidence we had in our possession. We started with the top bedroom, detailing its continued icy chill, the door being found constantly wedged open, my sighting of Alice, a lurid, full manifestation which then quickly disintegrated into thin air on my approach.

Examining the facts comprehensively, we came to the conclusion that young Alice must have unfortunately met her fate in that particular room, as it had almost certainly been her bedroom being the second oldest of the three. Her younger brother William Junior would inevitably have had the smallest.

"There must be a reason that the door has to be always continually open," I said thoughtfully as we scrutinised through the notes. "Maybe Alice was sexually abused in her room, on more than one occasion; the door being closed was a sign her father was shutting her in."

Together, we agreed with that synopsis; it seemed the only viable explanation.

We decided to move onto the smallest bedroom. I wrote down the appearance of the nasty monkey, playing offensively one minute then disappearing in the other. I shuddered, as my pen scribbled furiously on the pad, managing to once again, undeniably, creep me out. The unmade bed covers, with the dent in the pillow followed. There wasn't anything further that we could actually say about the room, other than it was possibly William Junior's. The despicable monkey had no relevance as far as we could see to anything; it just continued to scare me stupid.

For our bedroom, we listed Elisabeth's haunting vacant face appearing frequently at the window, staring blankly out with no emotion. Mark had been the first to see the full manifestation of Alice, staring expressionlessly at him in our doorway. Then we added the whispery shadows, and the final nail in the coffin, the camera having cleverly levitated itself from its propped position on the sweet-shop table downstairs.

Once again, we questioned the various paranormal occurrences for that room. Why was Elisabeth staring from that window in particular? Why had the camera been placed in the same spot on the windowsill? Reaching no sensible conclusions and thoroughly warmed up now,

Mark went to the bar and ordered our usual aperitifs, a welcomed compromise.

The refreshments clearly released our minds and slackened our tongues as our explanations became stupidly far-fetched and totally inexplicable. The authenticity of our situation finally managed to bring us down to much needed reality with a severely harsh bump. We began once more to concentrate in a far more serious manner, jotting down ideas and negating the less likely ones.

"I think that Elisabeth is showing us the window for a reason," I said, whilst doodling absentmindedly on our notes. "She is either waiting for someone to possibly arrive or maybe watching them leave." Together, we agreed that this was probably an accurate assumption, so I quickly highlighted the fact.

We could reach no verdict on why Alice appeared in the doorway that night, unless it was purely to spook us even further. The banging noises, we couldn't really put reasons to, and maybe they were only our creaky old cottage; realistically, they had certainly improved considerably since the ancient heating system had been replaced.

The children scampering about with their muffled laughter, we put down to the cottage being a village sweet shop in one of its former lives. Maybe it just so happened to attract every lost ghoul that hadn't yet 'passed over' and they regularly met to play in the den of paranormal pastimes. We managed to laugh at our mickey-taking humour, happy in the knowledge we were finding some sort of wittiness in our ludicrously farcical situation.

"I'm hungry; are you?" Mark said, changing the subject abruptly as he leaned back in his seat to read the menu.

"A little," I replied still totally enthralled with our increasing list of notes. "The stairwell is the place where most of the 'shadow people' seem to appear, even if it's the faintest whispery mist," I continued, as Mark proceeded to yawn loudly.

"Well, we know that Elisabeth was found hanging there, so that maybe explains why your handbag is moved onto the floor every night; it would undoubtedly have been the exact same spot she was found in. Someone or something is trying to direct our attention to that." Mark leaned forward as he spoke quietly. "Obviously, everyone knows for a fact that she hung herself, and we now have the knowledge that there is more to it, and maybe the handbag is showing us that."

I nodded, writing as quickly as possible. It was certainly a valid point, and I definitely couldn't think of anything more remotely sensible.

We decided to eat, much to Mark's absolute delight, and selfishly, it would save me from cooking later, so always an added bonus.

"Now that we have all these ideas, and if they are actually what our ghosts are trying to tell us, how do we go about telling them?" I asked my husband who was clearly concentrating more on his substantial plate of food.

"We could make up a Ouija board. Isn't that how you are supposed to communicate with 'the other side?' he said very seriously.

"No way are we doing that. I have read some horrific stuff about those things. They can attract demon monsters or evil spirits into your home if misused." I slammed my fork down in utter disgust, completely adamant with my unchangeable decision.

"Maybe you have been reading a tad too many horror stories." Mark laughed amusingly at my cross face.

"We could set the camera up again tonight, then leave our notes on the table. If they are clever enough to move things in our world, then surely they would be astute enough to read," I said in a sarcastic tone of voice.

"That's very true. We will put it in place again before we go to bed." He paused briefly, before continuing, "And if that doesn't work?" He stopped eating, waiting for my reply.

"If that doesn't work, we will have to see a priest. No more delays," I eventually stuttered, the words coming out in a solemn whisper. The harsh reality having once more sunk in, festering deep inside like a rotting corpse.

We finished the rest of our food in sombre silence. Inside, I felt pleased with our plan of action and confident that we were making some sort of headway. We gathered up our bits, and with Fred now awake and in full excitable action mode, we left the cheap pub satisfied that all was possibly in hand.

We walked Fred along the gusty seafront for twenty minutes before deciding to head home. Once again, I felt down at the prospect, like a huge black cloud endeavouring to cover me. Mark noticed my sudden change of mood and squeezed my hand tightly as we began the purposely slow drive home.

Darkness was creeping gently in as we pulled into the empty drive. The builders were thankfully gone. Mick had left a note, giving a brief rundown on the day's work, and more pleasingly wrote that tomorrow would be the last day.

"That's good news," Mark said, as he read the note out loud to me.

"Yes, it is," I replied, rapidly glancing around on the lookout for any apparitions or minor disturbances, not that I actually wanted to witness anything sinister at that moment in time.

We drank strong coffees as we wandered around examining our completed kitchen. The layer of dust had been, for once, efficiently cleaned by the workmen, obviously to display their fantastic craftsmanship which we couldn't fault. Our new cottage looked stunning. It was wonderfully perfect in every single way possible. The freshly painted walls and varnished woodworks looked brand new. The crisp white bathroom was near completion with just a small part of tiling and grouting to be concluded. There was just one thing tainting and spoiling what should have been our happy time; that was the distressingly bad nightmare that had unfortunately come with it.

CHAPTER TWENTY

We made it intentionally late, before deciding to go to bed, neither of us wanting to admit that we were probably more than just a little on edge with the bizarre situation. We spent half an hour precisely laying out our notes in an easily readable order. The camera was not only wedged solidly, but duct-tape encased completely with the books, making it a thoroughly secure vice. It would be an extremely difficult and demanding task trying to extract and release our weapon.

Completely satisfied with all our hard efforts, we followed each other upstairs, not wanting to make the walk alone. Like children, we undressed and used the bathroom in the presence of the other, soothing and comforting in the knowledge that help was respectively close to hand. We hastily climbed into bed and cuddled with the duvet covers clamped tightly over our heads, both bodies sweating profusely like boiling furnaces, but unconditionally safe within our ridiculous fortress.

Surprisingly, I managed to sleep really well and woke to an empty bed. Hurriedly, I grabbed hold of my dressing gown and used the freshly painted bathroom. Walking apprehensively down the stairs, I looked over at Mark who was sitting disengaged at the table. The notes were as we had left them, completely untouched and in their exact positions. The camera was in Mark's hands.

"Was the camera where it should be?" I enquired quietly, looking at my husband's clearly alarmed and distressed face.

"Yes," he finally stammered.

"What's the matter, Mark? Is there anything on it?" I sat next to him. He looked visibly shaken, and it was scaring me. "Mark?" I questioned again urgently, after being met with a blank wall of silence.

"Yes, there is, but I don't want you to look at it," he replied firmly, clutching the camera tightly inwards towards his body, protectively.

"What is it, Mark? You have to show me," I pleaded desperately, as violent waves of nausea welled up rapidly inside me.

"No, I don't want you to," he replied sternly, shielding the camera even further.

"Mark, we are in this together; you have to show me," I almost shouted at my poor husband as he sighed heavily.

Eventually, after what seemed an absolute eternity and with restrained hesitation, he haltingly moved the camera from his shielding body, and with uncertainty, he flicked the play button.

We both sat staring motionless at the unmoving image; the intense darkness of the room eerie and forbiddingly quiet, the ominous whir of the recording being the only solitary sound present. Abruptly, a shuffling commotion broke the unnerving deadlock of silence. The handbag was still sitting sedately in place on centre stage, the half-visible staircase still empty. Then for a split second the screen went grainy dark. I strained my eyes trying to identify anything more. Suddenly and without warning, two piercingly dark, golden-edged eyes filled the screen unexpectedly, causing me to jolt violently backwards in sheer terror. Not even a moment later, the screen returned back to the handbag and stairwell, the unsettling silences prevailing once more.

"That's it; I'm not staying here any more," I managed to mouth, as my whole body was recoiling in utter shock. I was shaking uncontrollably, my stomach reacting with steadily worsening waves of nauseousness.

"Okay, let's get our bits together. We'll find a B&B to stay tonight. Mick's going to be here soon; we'll make our excuses then go. First port of call is going to be the church."

Determinedly, Mark stood up, and together we almost ran upstairs, leaving our neglected and half-starved, confused little pup at the bottom. It took only minutes for us to pack overnight bags. I was in no mood to loiter, keener than ever to escape our house of horrors. Mark packed our stuff into the car, whilst I quickly saw to Fred's increasingly urgent needs.

Mick arrived to complete his remaining work in the bathroom; he also handed over as promised his final invoice for payment. Gerry the silent decorator arrived promptly to finish his final bits off, and both were promised payment over the weekend. I could barely concentrate as they spoke, hardly listening to or comprehending a single word that either of them had to say. All I could think about was those horrible devil-like eyes staring out of the camera lens, the nasty monkey now having absolutely zero effect on me in comparison.

Giving firm instructions to whomever left the property last to secure and lock all doors and windows, we drove off hurriedly, both of us fairly pleased to be leaving the cottage of terrors behind. In our haste, we managed to forget the dreaded camera and had to return to pick it up; it contained the crucial key to our evidence. Mark pulled up opposite the cottage and quickly ran in. I was frightened to even look up at our bedroom window, but something inside me was telling me to, drawing me in. I awkwardly craned my neck over to the driver's side and strained myself to look up; Elisabeth's haunting face stared out, this time her hand was touching the window, her fingertips dragging down the glass in exaggerated slow motion. I shuddered in fear as the iridescent image gradually shimmered away. A couple of minutes later, Mark returned to the car, and I recalled what just happened.

Deciding it was probably a little early to burden ourselves and, what would be perceived as, our far-fetched problem on the church, we drove slowly along and parked in the high street. Walking with Fred along the cobblestones to the café, we ordered two coffees. I was still shaking, apprehensive of what the future was now going to hold. I didn't want to live in that house ever again. I felt terrified, and although Mark didn't show much emotionally, I knew in my heart he felt the same.

We sat for a while mostly in a muted silence, grateful for the comfort that our cups of coffee had bought us. I quickly googled on my phone for B&Bs in and around our local area. Not many had dog friendly as a criterion. I gave up, knowing that we were both anxious to get the next part of the day out of the way. I felt extremely apprehensive, my mind full of trepidation and fear for the unknown.

Finishing our hot drinks, we returned to the car. Knowing vaguely the whereabouts of the church, we drove slowly down a tiny lane, hoping in anticipation that it may lead us to the entrance. Around five minutes later, we reached the gravel driveway, leading us into the surroundings of the daunting church and cemetery. We parked, and locking the doors, we walked Fred around the grounds, my bag heavily laden with my journal and evidence.

The imposing listed building was probably built around the 14th century, and many of the crypts and tombs we noticed were dated around this period. The gothic-style headstones stood crookedly, wear and tear over the years having clearly taken its toll. The graveyard was haunting, even in the early morning. Rays of sun trying to make their way through the clouds, bouncing beams scattering the deathly hallows, it almost felt like an unseen presence circling around us.

There was a slight mist in the air, which eerily seemed to linger spookily around the gravestones like wispy talons draping themselves over the creepy memorials. The whole place was petrifying even in the day. I shuddered at the thought of it at night, with all the fleeting shadows and the walking dead lurking about in the moonlight.

My mind in a turmoil of terror and in a woefully dismal place, I suddenly felt a gentle tap on the shoulder, which in my current state of frenzied paranoia, caused me to literally jump out of my skin. I turned around sharply, ready to face my demons. My eyes, however, met with a tall, middle-aged man with dark hair, speckled with flecks of silver. He was dressed in a floor-length robe, his dark eyes fixed onto mine in a non-confrontational way.

"Can I help you at all?" he asked in a calming polite manner.

"Oh, oh, I'm sorry." Apologising profusely, I continued, "We are looking for the Vicar," my voice sounding incredibly stupid and naive. Instantaneously, I also realised it was more than probably him, given his attire.

"Fortunately, you have found him. I am Father John," he kindly introduced himself, extending out his hand in greeting.

Politely, Mark and I shook his hand.

He continued, eyes fixed upon mine as he spoke; "And what is it that brings you to our humble church today?"

Mark spoke nervously, as Father John's gaze now transfixed in his direction. "I'm Mark, and this is my wife, Ann." He paused momentarily. "We have something personal and, to be quite honest, extremely strange that we would like to discuss with you, Father." Mark paused apprehensively, waiting for the Vicar's response.

"I have some spare time now, if you like; come this way," he replied kindly, bending down to acknowledge Fred. "Bring the little fellow too."

"Are you sure that's okay?" Mark almost stuttered.

"Yes, of course; please follow me."

We followed Father John to the small, pretty stone cottage attached to the rear of the old church. Passing the car on the way, we collected the remaining evidence in readiness. We entered the kitchen through a heavy wooden door which would have definitely been made in the medieval times.

We both sat nervously on miniscule wooden stools in the small stone kitchen. I looked around. It consisted of the simplest of amenities, as if it was almost a test of survival. The old-fashioned palette of the surroundings was insipidly bland, the air around engulfed in a musty stale odour. We fidgeted, anxious and filled with trepidation to begin our incredible testimony.

Father John delayed our mission even further by pouring us strong cups of tea. After an eternity, he sat down in front of us. Folding his arms on the table in front of him, he calmly asked us to begin.

Hesitantly, I looked at Mark. He nodded, encouraging me to begin. I almost stammered as I started with the sounds of the children playing next door, in a house that was supposedly empty, continuing to the handbag transporting every night, the fleeting glimmers of the 'shadow people' and my initial fruitless visit to our neighbours.

Father John sat listening, his face showing no signs of emotion, just seemingly concentration. I paused, waiting for a reaction. He waved his hand. "Continue, please."

I went on to explain the manifestation of the little girl we believed to be Alice in the top icy cold bedroom with the obstinate door, and subsequently, following her to the smallest bedroom where she led me to the awful encounter with the ghastly disappearing monkey.

Mark took over at that point as I became increasingly upset, pent up tears rolling uncontrollably down my cheeks. He then explained that he had been the first to see Alice standing in the bedroom doorway. I then interrupted, relaying the story of the unmade bed, trying to pass on as much information as possible. Gathering up strength, I brushed away my annoying tears and told of Elisabeth's hauntingly vacant face at our bedroom window each time we left.

Slowly and hesitantly, we relayed our confession, gaining more confidence as the story unfolded. We displayed the photographs and went through every piece of research that we had in our possession, including the admission from Freida that William was in fact her father and the story which our builder Mick had managed to extract from his elderly aunt. Each of us described in as much detail as we possibly could our individual encounters; both of us becoming visibly upset at different periods as the recollections undoubtedly disturbed us.

Father John continued to listen patiently, asking us gently to repeat certain parts and probing further where necessary to clarify events clearly.

We then went on to explain our elaborate plan to capture as evidence the images of the handbag moving, detailing the two failed attempts, the camera being tampered with and then being placed upstairs in Elisabeth's spot in our bedroom. Mark proceeded to take the camera out of my bag and asked Father John to look at the images from last night. We watched, uneasily, the impassive vicar in silence as he stared fully composed at the screen, his eyes opening widely in shock as the sight of the demonic dark eyes reflected out at him. Placing the camera on the table firmly, he pursed his lips together, almost whistling as he did so.

We sat in a prolonged unbearable silence, whilst he shut his eyes, taking a few minutes to dissect our tale. I glanced sideways at Mark who looked as anxious as I was.

Father John then finally spoke, breaking the endless morbid silence. "I would like to come and visit the cottage with you. I want to feel the atmosphere for myself. It sounds to me as though you have a clear-cut case of haunting. A spirit is something that continues to exist in some form after its physical body has passed on. Causes are usually unfinished business in their previous life or sudden or traumatic deaths, which indeed sounds to be the case of Elisabeth and young Alice."

He paused briefly before continuing, "I am no expert in the field of exorcism, and we, as priests, undergo very little training to aid us in matters such as these. Whilst we learn a great deal about the devil and the risks of manifestations of evil, exorcism is not a specialised area of study in seminary school."

He stopped momentarily, taking a deep breath. "I have access to the rite of exorcism which is an official document detailing the prayers and steps of exorcism. I will call on this to aid me. Are you in agreement with what I have to say?" He looked at us both.

I started to sob uncontrollably.

"We are," Mark whispered, tears welling up in his own eyes.

"Good. Do you understand exorcism? I will explain anyway. Exorcism is Greek for binding by oath; it is the religious practice of evicting demons or other spiritual entities from either a person or place." He paused, before continuing; "It's an ancient ritual and part of the belief system of many cultures."

"Thank you for believing in us, Father." I began to cry more, my tears cascading uncontrollably in sheer relief that maybe there was a ray of light at the end of the tunnel.

"My job is to have faith in everyone," he replied kindly. "I will come tomorrow at midday if that is convenient with yourselves?"

We both nodded in mutual agreement.

Father John continued on, "I will assess fully the situation, hopefully, gain an insight and feel for what sinister happenings are going on. We will then decide our plan of action from there. Now if you don't mind, I have some preparations to be getting on with." With that he stood up and shook our hands firmly. He placed his hand on my back as a source of comfort, and almost immediately, I felt as if God had been released into my soul.

We bade Father John a grateful farewell. Walking slowly through the churchyard, it now felt a much friendlier and safe place, nowhere near so intimidating. We drove back towards the town to begin our search for a dog-friendly B&B.

"Father John was absolutely amazing, wasn't he?" I looked at Mark as he drove.

"He seemed like a good chap. If he can actually help us, then even better."

"And if he can't?" I questioned dismally.

"He will. You must think more positively, Ann."

We spent over an hour trying to locate a dog-friendly room for the night, and eventually came across a large Georgian-style house nestled into the pine cliff tops, its white facade peering out amongst the vast expanse of trees. We knocked on the huge, pillar-framed front door, and after a short while a smartly dressed lady in her early sixties came to the entrance. We explained briefly that we had recently moved into the neighbouring village and were just looking for a room for the night whilst some inconvenient renovations were being carried out.

The lady, or Mrs White as she preferred to be called, welcomed us into her magnificent house. She went on to show us two exquisite rooms, both with stunning sea views. We chose the one with a beautiful window seat, somewhere we could just sit and take in the glorious, breathtaking, panoramic outlook. After paying her upfront, she explained the entry and exit procedures, asked us what time we would prefer breakfast and then proceeded to leave us to our own devices.

We sat on the pretty window seat, staring out at the rough, choppy sea. I lifted a confused Fred onto my lap, and he looked out in utter fascination, like us momentarily enjoying the picturesque landscape. The room itself was primrose yellow in colour and had a huge superior size bed covered in elaborate gold satin. There was a small seating area which housed a stripy Victorian-style sofa, a delicately small coffee table and a large TV. It was lovely; more importantly we could relax tonight.

Tomorrow was going to be an important day, the start of hopefully freeing our home from its sinister inhabitants. I found myself thinking about what Father John had said. He had more or less reiterated everything in detail that I had researched myself, although it had been good for Mark to hear it first-hand too. I looked at my husband. He looked peaceful and relaxed, his brow in the not so permanently furrowed state. The odd events of the past week had been hard on us both; it certainly showed today, when I saw the tears welling up in my husband's eyes as he recalled the strange occurrences to Father John.

I left Fred with Mark, both content and staring vacantly out the window. Unpacking our almost empty bags and placing Fred's bed in the corner on the other side of the room, I glanced around out our temporary surroundings. It felt homely and safe. Noticing tea and coffee making facilities in a cupboard, I took the opportunity of making a cup, and we sat silently sipping at our hot drinks. Fred explored the room, happy with his comfy bed in the corner. It was gone lunchtime so we decided to take our inquisitive puppy for another of his big walks, and from there we would eat out, probably in the dog-friendly, cheap pub which ticked all the right boxes.

We wrapped up and took a different walk over the other side of the cliff. Our B&B being so high up, we took advantage of its elevated position. The roads twisted and twirled around, like a never-ending maze. Neither of us had any idea where we were going or where in fact we would end up.

Walking for what seemed like miles, I couldn't decide if the hard, taxing, mountain terrain of the blowy cliff tops or the strenuous steep gradients of the B&B cliff were worse to negotiate. Still, it was nice to look at the variety of different properties scaling the edges of the treelined roads, the sea peeking out from time to time between the sometimes-colonial houses. A fine mist of rain started to fall. I put my hood up as the drops began to get persistently heavier. We found a huge tree where we sought temporary refuge, shielding us from the now sudden onslaught of heavy rain.

Fred was far from amused as his chubby little body continuingly shook to try to rid himself of the unwanted deluge of wetness. The rain, fortunately subsided, so we decided to take full advantage of the now brightening gap forming in the clouds to begin the mammoth task of trying to find our way back down towards the town.

Conveniently, we stumbled across a man-made path, which snaked itself cleverly down the cliffside, making a difficult walk so much easier. Fred was struggling now, as we made the descent downwards. Avoiding even the slightest puddles, he started to drag his backside obstinately at every available opportunity. Selfishly, I wanted him to be exhausted so that he wouldn't be a nuisance at our host's house. The walk was a lot longer than we had anticipated, all of us feeling the weary effects of the climb. It crossed my mind as we conquered the base camp that we would have to reach the summit once more a bit later on.

Arriving at the cheap pub, like the sad regulars that we were beginning to be, we managed to retain our corner booth table. Fred wearily dragged his damp body into the comfort of his portable bed. I wrapped him like a baby in his cot, and seconds later, he was in oblivion, his increasingly loud snores sounding weird from under the tranquil realms of the table.

I felt totally relaxed for the first time in ages. The stress of our initial move, the removals and the relocating had been challenging enough. Now with this abnormal presence ruining our lives and happiness, it had made everything so difficult to cope with. Having spoken to Father John earlier in the day, his calming demeanour had clearly worked wonders for us both; it had made us feel stronger inside. We now had an ally; more importantly, we had gained the help of God. I was never a churchgoer; in fact, neither of us was, believing, obnoxiously, that God was 'there' if you needed him. Now however, we needed him at all costs.

The first drink disappeared almost instantly, both of us treating it like an all-inclusive holiday; the only thing missing was our florescent wrist bands. Mark was now totally and utterly relaxed, making the most of the stress-free environment surrounding us. He was my tower of strength at the times when I was at my lowest; I sometimes forget that he might need some support too. Both of us going through this horrific ordeal, we needed times like this to allow us to reflect on matters and take stock of what was really important to us.

In a strange way, it felt like a mini holiday even if we were only in the town centre drinking cheap, budget-priced drinks and choosing food from the cut-price menu. Fred continued to snore out of sight under the table as we tucked into our economical meals, which were extremely good value and surprisingly tasty. Feeling full, we sat back in our private booth and chatted about the day's events and Father John in particular.

"Do you think Father will be able to help us?" I questioned Mark thoughtfully.

"I'm sure he's capable. I know that he said he wasn't trained or experienced in that field, but I'm pretty confident he'll do his best for us," Mark replied earnestly.

"Me too," I said agreeing. "I'm still feeling a little apprehensive about tomorrow; I don't want it to bring us false hope."

"We have to believe in Father John; we have no choice." Mark touched my hand reassuringly.

We decided to have one last drink before setting off on our hike up the evil cliff. I wasn't even sure that we would be able to find our way back, as we had stumbled across the path down by accident. I sipped at my wine, pleased of the numbing feeling it was having on me, completely relaxing my overly cautious and wary mind.

Mark was gulping back his Guiness like it was going out of fashion; clearly the desired effects were working on him too.

The escapism was a wonderful feeling, the relentless fear of the unknown, constantly rearing its ugly head as I tried so desperately every day to push it into the innermost depths of my most mind. It felt as though I had a permanent headache, with me continuing to fight off the enemy within.

Mark disappeared outside to smoke a cigarette. Although he was being strong for us, I could tell that he was uncomfortable with the whole unnatural situation that we had unfortunately found ourselves facing. It wasn't exactly normal everyday business, and most people would probably laugh in our faces if we even raised the unbelievable subject. I wondered how many others had experienced what we had. My smoky husband returned together with two more drinks. I felt decidedly tipsy as he plonked them down on the table.

"Are you trying to get me drunk?" I laughed, as he slumped heavily into the booth.

"Would I do that?" he replied, cheekily winking at me.

We finally finished our drinks, and I literally had to drag my disappointed husband up as he begged and pleaded like a child for another refill. With both of us staggering to the door and Fred running around our legs like a raving looney, we embarked on our off-putting journey ahead, the mere thought of the towering cliff doing nothing to encourage us to walk even the slightest few steps.

After what seemed like an eternity, we found the pathway entrance at the base of what seemed like Mount Everest. We ambled up the first monotonous zigzag, stopping every now and then to admire the sparkling array of lights twinkling in the town and harbour. The glistening sea was calm and glinting in the whiteness of the half-moon. The higher we climbed, the more spectacular the view became, completely different at night from day, colourful lights spreading as far as the eye could see.

It was a total mission trying to negotiate the steep climb after one drink too many, giggling, as we stumbled along the never-ending winding path, dragging ourselves along the wooden handrail that lined the edges, just for extra support. Fred did twice the distance as we lurched back and forth, side to side. Eventually, the peak was in sight. That was all very well but neither of us had the slightest inkling of what direction to take at that point. We paused to think and remind our failing memories of which path we had taken on the way down. Deciding to go right, we continued to stagger along unfamiliar territory, not recognising anything on the way.

After a long sobering hour, we stopped and stared at a house which looked vaguely recognisable, peaking out at us from a bend in the road. I looked around trying to get my bearings, now desperate to find our charming B&B. The delightful surroundings of the luxurious room were calling me. Wishing inwardly that I hadn't consumed that last fateful glass of wine, I stared at the curve of road ahead. It seemed like the correct one, and so taking Mark's arm, we aimed for it, hoping that my inner compass had worked.

Turning fully around the corner, we had the welcome confirmation; there ahead was the wonderful sight of the glorious Georgian mansion. Fumbling as quietly as we could for the front door keys, we silently let ourselves in, hoping that we could return unnoticed to our room. The room key found its way to the lock finally, and we piled into our room like a herd of elephants. I laughed as we collapsed in a heap on the sumptuous bed. Fred made his way wearily to his bed in the corner, before polishing off the dish of fresh water that Mark had laid out for him.

We both undressed and lay watching an old black-and-white movie, absorbed in the nonsense of the badly acted story. I felt myself nodding off as the high-pitched voices coming from the screen disappeared into the distance.

CHAPTER TWENTY-ONE

We sat at a table for four, in the large sunny breakfast room. The only ones present, we enjoyed the charmingly tranquil surroundings. Mrs White took our orders for breakfast, with Mark choosing the traditional full English and myself salmon with scrambled eggs. The room, like our bedroom, commanded a stunning outlook of the magnificent coastline and sea. I could never imagine taking it for granted; it was breathtaking.

Our breakfasts arrived swiftly. Mrs White discreetly left us alone as we ate the food which was delicious and cooked to perfection. We drank a few glasses of freshly squeezed orange juice, both of us severely dehydrated from the previous night's irresponsible drinking. Unsurprisingly, I had slept like a log, the drone of the black-and-white movie singing to me like a lullaby. Both of us slept soundly, not waking until the sunshine streamed into our lovely room; we hadn't even bothered drawing the heavy drapes the night before, oblivious and uncaring to everything around.

We sat for a good while, enjoying our cups of tea and the peaceful surroundings, not really wanting to leave our little temporary haven of solitude; the realisation of what the day ahead was to bring, quickly settling in like a dark raincloud. Having possibly outstayed our welcome, Mrs

White returned and noisily cluttered around us, stacking our plates and stripping the table clean. Reluctantly, we left to pack up and tidy our room.

We departed shortly after, thanking our kind host. I looked back at the lovely house, not wanting to leave the sheltered sanctuary. Couldn't we just stay until it was all over?

Sadly, we loaded the car, before setting off on our unfortunate drive home. It was eleven o'clock, and we had an hour before Father John would hopefully begin the rescue from our harrowing nightmare. I felt terribly uneasy, not sure what the afternoon would present to us.

"Right then, let's get home and sort this thing out, once and for all," Mark said loudly as if trying to bravely scare off the ghostly ghouls from his car seat.

I looked out of the window pensively, as Mark drove our car slowly down the winding roads of the cliff. We had to believe in Father John and have all our upmost faith in him. If we didn't, then our ordeal would continue; the future happiness and dreams that we had craved would be forever out of reach.

We joined the main road, and the town soon vanished behind us; the signs to our village soon fell upon us. As the high street loomed into sight, I felt physically sick; the vast amount of alcohol consumed the night before was also not helping. Arriving at our now picturesque cottage, the newly painted exterior looked appealing and pleasing to the eye, unlike the previous drab grey colour it was before.

For once, I made a conscious effort not to look up. Today we meant business, and nothing was going to stop us regaining the rightful possession of our own home. I didn't want to witness Elisabeth's haunting face at the window. I spoke loudly, not wanting to hear the children's muffled voices on entering. It worked, as I made a point of clattering around loudly.

Both of us seemed to be unintentionally mirroring the other's actions, busily tiding nothing in particular, fiddling about absentmindedly, with anything we could put our hands on. Trying to pass the time and keeping ourselves occupied, we bumbled around, and soon enough the time had come for our saviour's arrival. Waiting patiently, in a prolonged silence, we sat at the sweet-shop table, staring vacantly out at the road ahead.

Father John arrived exactly on time; he knocked sharply on the front door. Mark leapt quickly up and welcomed him inside. I wondered if Freida and Albert had noticed our ominous visitor as he had passed conspicuously by their house. I observed the priest taking a long deep breath on entering as he walked apprehensively into the front room. Extending my hand to him warmly, I offered a tea or coffee to which he politely declined.

"Could you show me around and point out all the areas which we spoke about yesterday," he almost whispered.

As we were congregated in the front room, we began there. I demonstrated the nightly manoeuvring act of the handbag, explained where the camera had been set up and pointed up the stairwell to where the fleeting images seemed to consistently manifest. From there we climbed the creaky staircase, where I continued to describe and demonstrate in detail the strange happenings that had been occurring. We entered our front bedroom, and walking over to the spot, I mirrored Elisabeth standing forlornly at the window. Mark then went on to explain his sighting in the doorway.

Father John remained extremely quiet throughout, his eyes examining each room intently. As we continued our tour up the hallway towards the top bedroom, I felt sure that the temperature had dropped somewhat in the house; it now seemed to have a prominent chill in the air. He seemed to hesitate slightly as we reached the icy chill of the doorway. The coldness of the air seemed to engulf us, absorbing itself rapidly into our pores. I turned to see Father John's frosty breath expelling into the atmosphere. He shuddered visibly.

We explained about the door being constantly wedged open on the uneven floor, a near impossible feat to occur on its own. I described the ongoing coldness in that room, which at that moment in time, we were all more than physically aware of. I could hear Father John's heavy breaths within the depths of his concentrated silence.

Progressing on and breaking the prolonged awkward hull, I explained that I had followed Alice's manifestation along the hallway, recounting my awful encounter with the hideous monkey which had, it seemed, vanished into thin air. Father John quietly followed us into the smallest room, where I pointed out the offending spot under the bed. Mark also mentioned us discovering the bed unmade which somehow managed to slip my mind.

Finally, we returned to the icy bedroom, where we gently opened the chests which we had unearthed in the musty loft space, pulling out items and photographs which could possibly aid our plight. After a while we replaced everything back into the chests.

"Shall we have a cup of tea now?" I suggested, keen to hear some sort of feedback on our unconventional presentation.

We sat for two further hours, drinking endless cups of tea and painstakingly going through each and every occurrence, remembering and adding to them as we recollected. Father John listened intensely, and with perpetual patience, he explained briefly what would happen. He had some further preparation to do prior to him returning to, hopefully, rid us of our haunting. Much to our disappointment, it was decided that he would return in two days.

Father John sensed our immediate dejection, explaining that he had to both mentally and physically prepare himself. Lots of homework was involved to ensure that he was in complete readiness for the task set ahead of him. Shortly after, Father John left us, shutting the door firmly behind him.

Mark gave me a cuddle. "Shall I call the B&B and see if she will have us for another couple of nights?"

"Maybe just tonight," I replied quickly. "It would be better if we were here the day before, don't you think?"

Mark nodded, dialling the B&B as I spoke.

Happily, our request was fulfilled. We arranged to pick up the key later, deciding to take a scenic drive along the coast and explore a little further afield.

CHAPTER TWENTY-TWO

We packed lightly again and took Fred out into the courtyard to do his business, to which he immediately obliged. Locking up the front doors, we left without a glance backwards, and headed southwards, letting ourselves quietly be enveloped in the peace and tranquillity of the calming picturesque drive. The sun was shining brightly, barely a cloud appearing in the light turquoise sky. The sea glistened in and out of view periodically, as we drove along the spectacular Jurassic coastline.

Driving in continued silence, our destination totally irrelevant, a mutual respect of the deep thoughts entwining between both our minds, we proceeded on. A fidgety and restless Fred made our decision for us. We pulled off onto a narrow coastal road, winding sharply in and out of the wall line, deep hedgerows. The low afternoon sun, flickering in and out of the landscape made the drive a little uncomfortable.

And then it happened: a van speeding unnecessarily around a sharp narrow contour, heading intimidatingly in our direction. Instincts told Mark to swerve, braking abruptly in unison with the incoming flash of van. Screeching, shattering sounds penetrated my head in what seemed like an eternal slow motion. I could hear a piercing scream cutting into the air, I realised in horror, it was my own; then everything went black.

My eyes opened. Blearily, I peered up trying desperately to focus on what was going on around me. Slowly, shapes and forms began to appear before my eyes. Realising that I was strapped onto a stretcher, I heard an ambulance lady calmly talking to me, gently holding and stroking my hand as I gradually began to come round. I felt her warmth sinking slowly into my skin. I strained my ears trying to hear her; everything seemed muffled and subdued.

"Ann, can you hear me?" I lip-read her words.

An inaudible sound escaped from my mouth.

"Ann, you have been in an accident. Try not to move."

I blinked to show her I was responding, her voice becoming increasingly clearer now.

"Mark? Mark?" I mouthed, panic consuming every single inch of me.

"Mark is okay. The firemen are here; they're cutting him from the vehicle. His leg is slightly trapped in the footwell. Please try not to worry; he is in very capable hands." She paused, before taking a call on her walkie-talkie. "We will be taking you to the hospital shortly. You have had, from what we can ascertain, a minor head injury, so are in a neck brace to restrict any further movement or damage as a precaution."

I was trying to take it all in. I just wanted to close my eyes; I felt so tired. "Fred? Our puppy?" I suddenly remembered, guilt washing over me at the same time.

"Don't worry about the little fella; one of the officers is making a huge fuss of him. We will make sure he is all right. Try to stay awake, Ann. We are going on our way now."

My arm hurt; my head was pounding. I was scared and wanted to see Mark. I started to cry, both in pain and in anguish, frustrated tears rolling down my face, feeling utterly sorry for myself.

The journey to the hospital was horrendous; every bump and turn rattled through my bruised bones. The painkiller they had administered was thankfully slowly taking effect. I managed to answer what seemed like endless questions, being far more compos mentis now. A police officer accompanied us on the journey, and I had given relevant contact details for Eve and Jennifer, together with my brief recollection of the moments before the accident.

After what seemed like a prolonged eternity, the ambulance arrived at the hospital, and I was transferred to the Accident and Emergency department. My kind ambulance lady bade me a fond farewell as she passed the handover paperwork to the awaiting team now surrounding me, promising adamantly that she would check up on me later.

A couple of hours passed, and I lay patiently waiting as different nurses came and went doing their various tests and monitoring. Mark, I was eventually informed, had been transferred to the same hospital and was currently being x-rayed. I asked, almost begged, if I could be taken to see him, but because it was confirmed that I had suffered a mild concussion, I had to rest. I felt utterly helpless and upset once more, wanting to just walk out and see him, but monitors and a drip line were attached, making an escape totally impossible. I shut my eyes, trying desperately to sleep, wanting this new nightmare to be over.

I woke, being surrounded by a group of doctors lining the sides of my bedside. One of them spoke, holding his file of notes in front of him. He went on to explain that I would be staying in overnight as a precautionary measure, having luckily escaped with a very minor concussion and bruising.

Mark, however, hadn't been so fortunate. He had suffered a fracture of the shinbone, the tibia, and was waiting to go into theatre imminently. The doctor assured me that it would be a relatively straightforward procedure, explaining that the surgeon would come to see me straight after the surgery with an update of how it all went. I felt frantic with worry, totally and utterly helpless, my inner self racked in hysterical frustration.

They left, moving on to the next bed in line. A nurse handed me my mobile phone, and I looked at the endless stream of missed calls from our children. I called each of them, explaining the awful day's events and the fact that Mark was currently in surgery. Eve wanted to get a flight straight home. We eventually came to a mutual agreement that she didn't need to unless something drastically changed. Jennifer arranged to come first thing in the morning as the evening now was rapidly drawing in. George was at university, and I explained that I'd keep him updated as soon as I knew anything. There was nothing any of us could do at the moment other than patiently wait.

Reassuring all three children, I felt completely drained emotionally and physically tired, my body battered and bruised. As I ended the last call, my thoughts turned to our home and then Father John. I suddenly panicked as the reality of the situation hurriedly began to sink in, wondering in distraught turmoil what we were to now do. I would need to call him tomorrow and explain our latest position. Once again, I felt lost and terribly alone. I looked at the hand, seemingly unmoving, of the clock on the wall. Time seemed to be stood still as I willed the hands to move around the sedentary clockface. Everything else seemed minor in comparison of what was more important to me right now.

Sorrow then returned to engulf my thoughts. *We shouldn't have moved,* I wailed loudly inside. Everything had been tainted in a dark black omen. What had been our beautiful dream was now shattered, literally in thousands of pieces around us. I found myself crying again, emotionally distraught at our decision to move, blaming myself for continually persisting to Mark that it was in our best interests.

Mark! I looked at the motionless clock again, as I pictured him sadly alone on the operating table. I wanted news. How long had it been now? Four hours or so? I stared angrily at the clock almost blaming it for the tiresome wait I was having to endure.

A sandwich and a jelly was put in front of me. I couldn't face eating, nausea going backwards and forwards in tidal waves inside me. I wasn't sure if it was the worry or the trauma medication that was being regularly administered. I pushed it to one side. It was covered with clingfilm; I could eat it later if I felt hungry.

My mind began racing erratically again, flashbacks of the accident and our ghosts being merged into one continual horror movie. I needed to remain calm and focused. I couldn't concentrate on anything. The noisy hustle and bustle going on in droves around me put a stop to that. Every new person that walked by, I was fervently sure would be the surgeon arriving to give me news, only to be shrouded in disappointment like a hard kick in the stomach when they walked on by.

Again, the clock beckoned; it continued to irritate me immensely. I looked up yet again at the new figure now approaching me. A tall, dark-haired man in his early thirties walked purposefully to my bedside.

"Mrs Lee? I'm Doctor Vincent," he spoke, his calming manner sedating my almost frayed nerves.

"Yes," I replied, pulling myself up straight.

"Your husband has had his surgery; it was a straightforward fracture which fortunately didn't carry any unnecessary complications. He will be looking at around three to six months recovery period as I have had to insert a small internal rod during the procedure. He will then be in a cast for six weeks followed by a special boot. A course of probably ongoing physiotherapy will need to be completed to gain strength." He paused, waiting for my response.

"He's okay then?" I managed to numbly stutter.

"Yes, he's absolutely fine. He's out of the anaesthetic and back on the ward, all ready, asking for you." He smiled. "A nurse will be with you shortly to take you to see him." He patted my hand kindly.

"Oh, thank you so much." Tears began to flow again as my emotions took control again. "Thank you so much," I repeated.

"You're more than welcome," he responded sympathetically.

I breathed a deep sigh of welcomed relief. After a lengthy twenty-minute wait, spent again looking at the clock, a janitor pushing a wheelchair appeared; a nurse followed behind. She helped me from the bed and released my saline drip, which had almost finished anyway. Gently and carefully, I was pushed through a cold corridor to a lift which took us up two floors to a ward almost identical to the one I had just left.

I couldn't wait to see my husband, feelings of love completely overwhelming me. We turned into a room of four beds, and there he was, leg raised into an uncomfortable looking hoist, the unflattering hospital gown, mirroring mine. Other than the obvious injury to his leg, he looked well, with no visible bruising in sight.

"Mark," I almost wailed.

His face lit up, and he smiled broadly, holding out his hand towards me. I reached out for it and stretched awkwardly to kiss him, as tears once again fell in bottomless cascades.

"It's okay, I'm fine. No tears. How are you?"

I explained that other than a little concussion and bruising, I was good – other than emotionally – and being released the next day as a precautionary measure.

"I was worried sick about you," he replied, gently stroking my hair. I felt like a small child being comforted.

We spoke for over an hour, the nurses kindly allowing us extended time. Mark had complete recollection of the accident, saying that the reckless driving of the van driver had contributed to causing the unfortunate catastrophe to inadvertently happen. The police had reportedly arrested the uninjured driver at the scene.

Tiredness suddenly overcame both of us, the exhaustion from the long, awful day quickly enveloping us. I was returned to my ward, where I fell asleep instantaneously, comforted in the fact that Mark was fine.

CHAPTER TWENTY-THREE

Jen arrived the next morning and waited with me whilst the doctors completed the appropriate release paperwork. It had been a long and disrupted night, the noisy bustle of the ward ongoing and uncaring about its patients trying to sleep. I had woken almost every hour and found myself staring constantly at the annoying clock willing it to be morning. Finally, after yet another prolonged waiting period, I was released.

We made our way to the lift and took it the two floors up to see Mark. He was sat up in bed looking a lot brighter than the previous night. He'd managed to sleep well even with all the continuing disturbance of his surroundings. His surgeon had already checked on him and was pleased with how everything was.

We stayed for a short while, very conscious of the fact I had lots to sort out. Earlier, I had sent a message to Father John explaining our unpleasant predicament. A kind reply quickly followed, asking me to call him when convenient. He also added a promise that he would include us in his daily prayers.

On our way home, I decided to tell Jen about our ghostly encounters. She was totally horrified, but at the same time extremely intrigued. I think she struggled to take it all in, as I babbled the story out to her, shaking her head in disbelief and scepticism. She was endeavouring to stay a few days; therefore, it was imperative that she knew our situation.

Our first port of call was the police dog pound, where we found our little man looking tremendously forlorn and sorry for himself, his little features crestfallen.

"Oh, Fred." I quickly scooped him up into my arms, his little body shaking in happiness. He appeared to be genuinely smiling as he went on to lick me stupid. Holding him tight, we took him to Jen's car. I hoped he wouldn't be nervous, but he was oblivious as I cuddled him reassuringly on my lap until we were home.

Opening the front door dubiously, the fresh paint smell overwhelmingly filled the air. I swiftly looked around, my eyes darting this way and that. Everything seemed normal and in order. I sensed no feelings of forbode or dread, which comforted me somewhat. The kettle rattled noisily as I showed Jen the beautiful work that had been completed since she previously visited us.

"It looks lovely, Mum," she commented taking it all in as we walked slowly around. "Why don't I run up the deli and get us a baguette or something whilst you make the tea?" she added enthusiastically.

I felt guilty, realising she wouldn't have eaten all morning after having driven for a long time. "That's a great idea," I replied, suddenly aware of my own hunger pains gnawing away inside me. I had barely eaten for two days and now felt decidedly ravenous.

Jen returned, arms laden with freshly baked cheese and salad baguettes. We sat at the sweet-shop table, both of us enjoying the delicious offering in front of us.

Whilst she had been gone, I'd gathered together the details of our insurance company. Our car which had been towed away at the scene, seemingly, would appear to have been written off. After a laborious hour-long phone call, of which details and circumstances to the best of my knowledge had been passed over, it was arranged that a courtesy car would be delivered to me the following morning.

I felt momentarily relieved that everything was now in order, other than our ghosts who I secretly and ridiculously hoped would have feelings and remain out of sight for a while. Jen with impeccable timing, seemed to have read my thoughts and raised a few questions about them. I showed her my pile of evidence, which she sat and read intently as I explained and pointed out the various sightings. I went on to show her the grainy photographs which we had managed to identify.

"Well, I am definitely sleeping in your bed with you!" she joked, at the same time deadly serious.

"I thought you might." I nodded, secretly appreciating the fact that I didn't need to sleep alone.

We took Fred out into the courtyard and fed him before leaving to return to the hospital with the long list of things Mark had requested to have brought in. The hospital fortunately wasn't far away, and twenty-five minutes later, we were making our way once again to the lift. He smiled immediately as he saw us walk into the ward.

"Hello you," I said, kissing him gently on the forehead. "How are you feeling?"

"A bit sore. The pain killers are helping though, just making me feel a little sleepy," he replied.

Jen bent down to kiss his cheek.

"Hello. love," he warmly greeted her.

We unpacked his pyjamas so that he was able to change from the unflattering and uncomfortable hospital gown. They would probably have to be cut to fit his cumbersome plaster. His charger and iPad, I placed within reach on the manoeuvrable table in front of him. We had picked up some magazines and toiletries on the way, together with some soft drinks, fruit and snacks.

"Oh wow. Thank you, darling." He squeezed my hand gently.

We stayed a couple of hours, Mark clearly tiring towards the end of our visit. I had updated him on everything I could including my message to Father John.

"What should we do about that?" he had asked.

"I will arrange for him to come as soon as Jen leaves," I responded, having already decided this.

Mark nodded his approval before yawning loudly.

We left shortly after and decided on our drive back that we would eat out, both of us choosing the hotel which we could walk to. Rather than disturbing Fred, we pulled straight onto the drive and walked up the cobblestone street towards the hotel. I felt hungry again and selfishly was pleased that I didn't have to put together a meal, motivation and energy severely lacking.

We sat at mine and Mark's usual table. Fleetingly, I felt a pang of loss that he wasn't with me. It was a strange situation, and if it wasn't for Jen sitting opposite me, I would have burst into floods of tears.

Noticing my glistening eyes, she patted my arm gently. "It's okay, Mum, everything will be fine." She had clearly noticed my obvious upset.

"I know," I quickly replied, my cheeks flushing furiously. "Just feels odd without Mark here."

I picked up the menu and handed it to her. We spent a few minutes browsing. Before the waitress politely took our orders, she asked where Mark was as it was highly unusual for me to be seen without him. She was shocked as I explained briefly what had happened. A few minutes later she returned with a bottle of crisp white wine. I quickly gulped down a mouthful, appreciating the relaxation it was now expertly providing me.

We chatted over dinner, enjoying the one-to-one time that we were actually spending together, a rarity in itself. Both our meals were delicious as always, and Jen chose a dessert which we shared as the portion size was so immense. It was a lovely evening with us both enjoying the others company. I felt so much better, probably due to the numbing effect of the wine.

We walked home in a satisfied silence, and on entering the cottage, I heard the children which Jen thankfully, it seemed, was oblivious to. We saw to Fred before going up to bed, giving him lots of cuddles and affection, much to his unfaltering delight. I left the hall light on for comfort, and we both hid inadvertently beneath the covers, grateful for the others presence.

I woke first, having surprisingly had a peaceful uninterrupted sleep. Jen was cocooned like a sausage roll, so I left her to continue her slumber. It was early, and the birds were proudly singing their dawn chorus. I went downstairs, and for once, everything was as it should be. Fred looked up wearily, as I bent down to stroke him, and within seconds was up and about bounding around happily. I fed him his breakfast, and he noisily pushed the bowl around the kitchen like a greedy little piglet, grunting and groaning as he ate. Having licked his bowl clean, he took himself out into the courtyard, sunrise slowly creeping in.

I made a cup of tea and sat staring in silence at the outside world, contemplating the day ahead and my plan of action with our unwanted guests. I messaged Father John conscious of the early hour, but totally focused on my mission to get things underway. Jen was departing the next day, so ideally, I needed it resolved then. Surprisingly, my phone vibrated immediately, and Father John confirmed he would arrive at eleven thirty the next morning. I smiled, pleased that it had been arranged so promptly.

I decided to take Jen to the town so that we could leisurely browse around the shops, killing some time before we were able to visit Mark again during the afternoon visiting slot. My phone vibrated again. Mark had replied to my text of 'good morning'. We conversed backwards and forwards, with another list of requests sent my way.

Jen woke at nine. We had a light breakfast of cereal and toast. She liked the idea of going into town, shopping being one of her favourite pastimes. Finishing, I tidied the table and washed up whilst Jen used the bathroom. I shouted up to her that I was taking Fred out for a quick walk.

Gathering his little harness and lead, I managed to put them on with his body shaking in happiness. Closing the front door behind me, I glanced up out of habit at the bedroom window. I fleetingly thought I saw the curtain move. Brushing it quickly to one side, I started to walk Fred at a speedy pace, breathing in the exhilarating fresh damp air as we went.

I returned a while later, and having tucked an exhausted Fred in his bed, we left the cottage with Jen driving us into town. Frustratedly, the courtesy car that had been due to arrive was now coming at eight thirty the next day.

We parked by the sea and walked for a bit along the seafront, the sharp wind always embracing. There was something about the sea and its sometimes-violent waves that always managed to clear my head and thoughts, allowing me to embrace the peace and tranquillity the coastline had to offer.

"It's lovely here, Mum; it was a good choice to move," Jen said smiling, as she stared nonchalantly out to sea.

"I have questioned that so much over the past couple of days, I'm afraid," I responded wistfully.

I'd told her over breakfast that Father John was coming. She had wanted to stay, but I hastily declined her eager offer as it was something that was to be done alone.

We continued along, until the colourful beach huts loomed into sight. At that point we turned left towards the town and strolled unhurriedly along the shop-lined boulevard. I think we must have visited each and every shop for what had seemed like hours, Jen being in her total element, picking up and putting down an array of possible items to purchase. By the end she could barely carry the vast number of bags she had seemed to expertly accumulate. I had Mark's list of requirements to concentrate on, which unbelievingly, I'd managed to obtain in between the quirky boutiques.

"Let's grab a coffee and a sandwich before we leave for the hospital," I said as we headed in agreement towards a pavement café.

We both ordered creamy lattes, together with cheese and tomato paninis, which were absolutely delicious. The café was bustling with happy chatter and laughter; it gave me a much needed warm and welcoming feeling inside. It had been a thoroughly enjoyable way to pass the morning, and Jen was babbling on excitedly about her bottomless purchases.

Arms heavily laden, we walked back to the car, having wished fervently that we had parked nearer to the town centre. Fingers red raw from carrying too many bags, we finally arrived at the carpark, and being somewhat relieved, unloaded the shopping into the boot. I filtered out Mark's bag of requests and put it into the front footwell with me. We then took the road out of town towards the hospital with Jen continuingly chattering nineteen to the dozen.

CHAPTER TWENTY-FOUR

Pulling up in the overly congested hospital car park, I gathered the bag of Mark's supplies whilst Jen visited the extortionate pay and display machine. We walked the usual route to the lift. Mark's face lit up as soon as we walked in; annoyingly, my eyes welled up the moment I saw his happy-to-see-us face.

He updated us on anything and everything relevant. The doctors had informed him earlier that he was making excellent progress which was a massive relief. We spent the rest of the afternoon talking about nothing in particular, various nurses coming and going and adding to Mark's ever expanding medical notes.

In the next bed was a young chap who had also suffered a leg fracture. The pair of them had struck up a pleasant relationship with plenty of banter firing backwards and forwards. It made the long day far more bearable for Mark, and he appreciated the young man's company.

Visiting time quickly drew to a rapid close. We bade our farewells, with Mark whispering, "Good luck for tomorrow," and asking me to message him immediately after.

A morbid sense of forbode engulfed me as we took the lift downstairs. Jen sensed my change in mood immediately, suggesting that we should stop on the way back for something to eat, her treat. We both agreed that this was a nice idea, and on the way back, we came across a small Italian restaurant and pulled into the car park.

We checked the menu on the wall in the entrance and decided that we would give it a try. There were a few other customers seated as we walked in. The front of house was an Italian lady who welcomed us like long-lost friends, quickly ushering us to a table in the window. We both decided to order home-cooked lasagna, having spotted it being delivered to an adjacent table.

The meal was lovely, with us both now being quite hungry. I made a mental note to bring Mark back there, when he was home, as the atmosphere and service was second to none. We paid our bill which was extremely reasonable, thanking the attentive hosts as we left. I yawned as we began the final part of the drive home. It had been a long day, and the thought of the morning terrified me.

I made cups of tea, and we sat quietly watching the TV as Fred bounded happily around, pleased that once again he had company. My phone vibrated as a message came through from Father John. I panicked, thinking that he would be cancelling. I needn't have worried as he was confirming once more that he would be here. My mind, then went into overdrive with apprehensive, negative thoughts taking over every empty space of my head, whirling feelings of panic and dread engulfing every part of my body. I tried to focus on the TV, the muffled sounds coming from the screen meaning nothing to me. In the background I heard Jen speaking; I snapped hurriedly back out of my traumatised state, realising that she was telling me she was tired and going to bed.

Fred went outside in the darkness of the courtyard as I tidied away our cups. Nestling him quietly into the comfort of his little warm bed, I followed Jen upstairs, hoping and praying that I would be able to sleep.

CHAPTER TWENTY-FIVE

Morning came with a beam of sunshine filtering through a tiny gap in the curtains. I glanced at the clock beside me; it was six thirty. Surprisingly, my sleep had been quite decent, probably due to the long, tiring and emotional days. Jen was snoring gently as I left the bedroom to go to the bathroom.

As I walked downstairs, out of habit, I automatically looked at the handbag spot. Nothing was going to be different as I had purposely hidden my bag away in a kitchen cupboard. I felt myself smirking at my cleverness. On seeing me appear, Fred leapt out of his bed like a deranged looney, his chubby little body dancing around in circles, knowing that he was about to be fed. I gave him a belly rub as he threw himself on his back, legs quivering upright in the air.

I returned upstairs and got dressed, oddly wondering what on earth to wear for the occasion. I quickly pulled on some leggings and a jumper, satisfied with my simple look. Jen was in the shower, her mobile phone blaring out some sort of music. I went down to make us a bacon sandwich before she left.

Her company had been a welcome relief for me. We sat eating at the sweet-shop table, staring out at the road ahead. I helped load her bags into the car, and with Fred licking her face profusely, we said our goodbyes. My eyes welled up heavily as I watched her car fade into the distance.

As I was about to go back inside, the courtesy car turned up, a small red thing which would be adequate temporarily. I signed the necessary paperwork, having checked the car over with the delivery men. At least I would be able to visit Mark and get around, I thought, as they drove off.

I made myself busy in the house, tidying up and spring cleaning to cleanse my mind of untoward thoughts. Every time my head began to wander, I sang. Despite being full of trepidation, this was not the time to show it; I needed to be stronger than ever and rid my home of its demons.

At eleven fifteen, I sat nervously at the sweet-shop table, hands clasped in fists in my lap. I texted Mark who immediately replied, probably as anxious as I was. I couldn't wait for this day to be over.

CHAPTER TWENTY-SIX

Father John arrived exactly on time. As he passed the window, I noticed he was wearing the obligatory surplice and purple stole, the attire which performed part of the ritual. He knocked sharply on the front door. I quickly got up to let him in.

I offered a cup of tea or coffee to which he refused the offer, choosing instead to walk slowly around the bottom floor observing each room completely, his eyes taking everything in as we passed each room. I was sure that the temperature had dropped throughout the house; it seemed now to have a distinct chill in the air. Maybe it was my imagination, I thought, as we continued to peruse in deep silence.

Eventually, Father John asked me to explain again the exact points of manifestation and the areas that seemed to be the hot spots. Silently, he took it all in. I felt it was some sort of meditation, and it was unnerving me severely.

"The time has come for us to begin," he finally spoke in a quiet voice, whilst grasping firmly his book of prayers. "Whatever happens, I have to complete the ritual. You must remain calm throughout and take instructions from me," he continued firmly.

I nodded, feeling petrified at the thought of what was going to happen.

"Remember, we have to complete the procedure," he reiterated once again.

I followed the priest's powerful figure upstairs to the top bedroom. He advised that this was where the ritual would begin; it seemed to have the most presence about it. He told me to stand alongside the far wall as he closed the stiff door firmly behind him. The temperature was like ice; I definitely hadn't imagined it. I shivered uneasily, waiting for the unknown.

Father John stood in a trance-like state, staring intently at the open pages of his book, seemingly gaining strength from the words set out before his eyes. He placed a cross over the pages and stared upwards, breathing in the frosty air.

"Lord, have mercy," he began.

"Lord, have mercy." He beckoned me to repeat with him.

"Christ, have mercy."

Again, I repeated.

"Lord, have mercy."

"Christ, hear us."

"God, the Father in heaven."

"Have mercy on us."

I continued to repeat when Father John instructed me, my body now shaking visibly. He traced the sign of the cross over himself, me and the freezing room, reciting more prayers as he did so and sprinkling holy water all around the room.

"Our Father, Who art in heaven, hallowed be thy name; Thy kingdom come; Thy will be done on earth as it is in heaven.

"Give us this day our daily bread; and forgive us our trespasses as we forgive those who trespass against us; and lead us not into temptation, but deliver us from evil."

As Father John raised his cross, the rigid door banged open with an almighty force. Pointing the cross at the empty doorway, he continued, his voice much louder and commanding:

"God, whose nature is ever merciful and forgiving, accept our prayer that this servant of yours, bound by the fetters of sin, may be pardoned by your loving kindness."

I stood motionless and terrified; my hands having been clenched in fists were almost blue. My mouth was parched dry; I wasn't sure if it was the cold or the heavy breaths escaping from my arid mouth.

The door began rattling against the wall, banging louder and louder as Father John raised his voice, trying to overpower the increasing volume that the door was now making. My hairs stood on end as he strongly recited words from his book, continuing to sprinkle the holy water in the direction of the imposing doorway as he did so.

"I cast you out, unclean spirit, along with every satanic power of the enemy, every spectre from hell, and all your fell companions; in the name of our Lord Jesus Christ." He chanted repeatedly, as he traced the sign of the cross over himself and me.

I watched and listened in shock, horrified at the disturbing events happening around us, paralysed in fear and terror. The loft hatch started to bang, as Father John continued to recite, frosty air wisping from his blue lips as he spoke.

"Lord, heed my prayer.

"And let my cry be heard by you."

I repeated as instructed, my voice whimpering pathetically.

"The Lord be with you."

The banging continued to become louder, almost deafening. I could hear muffled children's screams; it was spine chilling as their wailing voices seemed to pierce through the shaking walls.

"Depart then, impious one. Depart, accursed one. Depart with all your deceits, for God has willed that man should be in his temple. Why do you still linger here? Give honour to God the Father almighty, before whom every knee must bow. Give place to the Jesus Christ who shed his most precious blood for man."

I followed Father John throughout the cottage, as he repeated the powerful words, reciting them loudly at the deafening knocking. The walls seemed to be shaking as I cowered behind his commanding figure. He led the way bravely, defying the almighty presence that had blatantly been disturbed.

Suddenly and unexpectedly, the banging stopped; it was eerily silent as we paused momentarily on the stairs. Father John proceeded to recite further, quietly and almost whispering the authoritative, holy words. He turned to face me as he raised his hand, drawing the sign of the cross over his own and my exhausted body, for what was to be the last time.

"Amen."

"Amen," I repeated, tears falling down both of our cheeks.

The temperature of the hallway had risen. It now felt surprisingly warm, and together in silence, we walked to the top room, where unusually the door was firmly shut.

Father John pushed the stiff door open; the room was quiet and warm. "Your spirits have gone," he said confidently, as we walked into the room.

I followed him in. I couldn't find any words to speak, as my eyes glanced around the previously unwelcoming room. The dark, heavy atmosphere had lifted from it, like heavy curtains that had now been pulled open. It felt fresh and warm, not the slightest chill present in the air. I ran over to the priest and rightly or wrongly hugged him, sobbing like a baby as I did so. Father John smiled kindly as he patted my shoulders, an unspoken bond now existed between us; we would be eternally in his debt.

"Now if you don't mind, I'll have that cup of coffee, and if you have a brandy, it would be very much appreciated." Father John smiled as he spoke, the colour now returning to his lips.

I shut the bedroom door behind us as we made our way downstairs, victors in our battle to regain possession. I made coffees and poured a glass of much-needed brandy, which managed to steady our frayed nerves. Still shaking like a leaf, I barely managed to drink from my mug, spilling coffee on the table in the process.

We sat and discussed what had occurred, the actual shock of the harrowing events slowly sinking in. Father John recommended that it would be healthy to discuss our experiences with each other or him anytime that we felt the need. More importantly, he reassured me that the evil had now left our home. Taking comfort from his kind words and the warming glasses of brandy, I thanked him repeatedly, forever grateful for his belief in the first place and finally his actions in dispersing the haunting from our home.

Leaving me alone, Father John said his goodbyes, promising that he would call the next day to make sure everything was all right. Shutting the door behind him, I stood motionless in the doorway as the tears began to flow again, emotions flooding out. It was an experience I never wanted to encounter again, the terrifying realisation of what we had been through engulfing my body and mind. I walked over to the table and called Mark.

CHAPTER TWENTY-SEVEN

I walked Fred down the lane, just to get some much-needed fresh air. Out of habit I stared apprehensively up at our bedroom window, fearing what image would meet my gaze. I worried unnecessarily as our curtain remained intact and no haunting face was peering out.

Walking Fred alongside the river, the fresh air worked wonders as I felt invigorated and strong once more. We had beaten the demons and could once more enjoy our new home and life as we should have been able. The shallow water gently trickled by as I stopped to take in the beauty that the picture-perfect riverside had to offer. Two ducks happily swimming side by side were rudely interrupted by Fred who decided he wanted to become their new playmate. Their romantic date disturbed, they fluttered along the top of the water in sheer panic, with an excited Fred in hot pursuit. I shouted at him, extracting his extendable lead. He returned, forlornly his big grey eyes making me feel guilty for halting his innocent play.

I continued along the riverbank, stopping every so often for our nosy little pup to explore strange and new plants or objects presenting new places to bury his flat little nose in, his little head stopping, sniffing, experiencing the new fragrances all around him.

Yellow and pink primroses were dotted prettily amongst the shrubs on the banks; the trees and bushes an exuberant array of autumnal colours, adding a lavish display to the landscape. Once again, I was reminded of the reason we had made the move, briefly forgetting the horrors that we had so undeservedly been put through.

I eventually arrived at the stile which would lead me back to the little lane near home. I climbed over it with ease, having done so many a time. Fred managed to tangle himself awkwardly, his extended lead now in knots. I held onto his wriggling frame as I freed his restricted little legs from the jumbled mess. I placed him back down, and we continued along the path, darkness now falling quickly around us.

Our cottage came into sight. I stared upwards and smiled as there was nothing there. No sounds of children greeted me as I walked in, silently this time, my ears listening for the slightest footstep or muffled voices. It was all fine, and on checking upstairs, the bedroom door had remained shut. We had our home back.

Mark called as soon as I stepped into the door. The doctors had been round and was to prepare his release paperwork in the morning. With the help of physio, he could continue his recovery from the comforts of his own home. Secretly and selfishly, I was overjoyed as despite the exorcism, I really wasn't looking forward to being home alone. We made arrangements for the following morning, and I put the phone down.

Staring slowly around at my surroundings, I tried to find something that was wrong, something out of the ordinary, but there were no fleeting glimpses, no muffled voices; everything seemed calm and in place. I went into the kitchen and made myself a cup of strong tea. Nestling into the sofa in front of the TV, I snuggled with Fred, glad of his canine company.

CHAPTER TWENTY-EIGHT

A few months passed quickly by. There had been no sight or sound of any weird manifestations, and no poltergeist activity. Our menacing demons had gone forever, and we began to enjoy settling into our new quiet home as we should have been able to have done initially. Fred was fractionally bigger, still comical and playful, although he had calmed down immensely. He was a good companion to have around, and we both loved everything about his funny little character.

When the exorcism had first been performed, we were both constantly looking out for the slightest thing which would allow us to say that our ghosts were back. The tiniest noise had me hushing my husband into silence, whilst we then craned our ears and eyes to locate the source. At night, I placed my handbag purposely in its spot on the sofa, just to see if it had been moved in the morning; it never was, and I soon gave up trying to trap something that clearly was no longer there.

The top bedroom door remained shut now, and the room always felt sunny and warm rather than the foreboding icy environment that it once was. The curtain in our bedroom never moved, and we both gave up looking, neither of us really wanting to witness anything again.

Father John not only became a frequent visitor to our home; he became our friend. Many a night the three of us would share a glass or two of brandy whilst we brought the world to rights. Although of late, we hadn't seen much of him, and when we did bump into him in the village, he had seemed a little pre-occupied. Unsurprisingly, we became avid churchgoers, taking comfort from the prayers that Father John spoke so well. Forever indebted to the church, our beliefs in God would now never die.

Mark joined the golf course, when I eventually let him out of my sight. At first it bothered me being left on my own in the cottage. Overcoming my wariness, I became stronger each and every time my husband went out. Initially, I wouldn't move from the sweet-shop window, waiting patiently to see his car return from wherever he had been. Now it didn't matter; I went about my day-to-day duties like any normal person would. I also began doing some voluntary work at the church, giving back some of my time in repayment of the help that we had so gratefully been given.

I think the children found it strange that the church now played an important part of our lives. Apart from Jen knowing, we had made the decision to keep quiet on our strange happenings; there was no point in scaring them unnecessarily. We had a wall of silence surrounding that part of our lives, with Father John and Mick the builder having the only knowledge. It was our secret and that was to be how it would remain.

CHAPTER TWENTY-NINE

Mark had returned from cleaning the car. We sat down to enjoy a candlelit meal for two. It was nearly Christmas, and we were looking forward to the arrival of the children in a couple of days. The Christmas tree looked beautiful in the corner, with silver tinsel and baubles covering it. Dazzling, iridescent white lights added to the shimmering effect with a pile of presents filling the stone floor beneath it.

Three sacks lay side by side, the same ones that the children had traditionally used since childhood. They still expected them to be filled on Christmas Eve, which they would be. Fred had a little Christmas stocking filled with doggy gifts; he guarded it heavily, sniffing and checking on it constantly. The cottage looked beautiful with its full Christmas decor; I had even placed a real tree in the sweet-shop window, prettily decorated for people passing to admire as they walked past.

I cleared the table and tidied the kitchen, before sitting down in front of the television. I sat staring at my decorated tree, approving vainly my own artwork. Mark watched golf as I bent down to pick up a magazine from the coffee table. All of a sudden there was a huge bang from upstairs. I jumped up screaming in shock, the noise startling the wits out of me.

"Mark?" I screamed in fright. "They're back!" I looked at him, terror taking hold rapidly.

"No, they are not," he replied. "Look." He pointed to the top of the staircase.

I looked nervously towards the top of the semi-dark stairwell. There Fred's fluffy head peered out through a gap in the wooden bannisters, a naughty, mischievous look on his seemingly, smiling face.

"Oh, Fred!" I said, sheer relief flooding through me.

I turned to Mark and we both laughed together, both relieved that our phantoms from the other side hadn't returned. Returning to the pages of my magazine, I paused, wondering if it would always be like this.